Conveyor B

A Ron Web

C000253007

Pete Jennings

Best wishes Pete

Gruff Books © 2021

12, Carlton Close, Gt. Yeldham

Halstead, Essex U.K. CO9 4QJ

Also in the Ron Webb mystery Series:
Dog Walk Detectives (Gruff Books - 2021)

This book is dedicated to my good friend Caroline Archer.

Chapter 1. Felixstowe, Suffolk. Wednesday, June 8th 2016.

56-year-old Sidney Button leant both elbows on his old oak desk and brought his fingertips together in front of his neat, grey beard with a sigh. He had a frown, and the worry lines on his forehead beneath his thinning hair deepened as he contemplated what he should do? Checking his watch, he calculated that it would be 11 am Eastern Standard Time in the USA. Checking the code and number, he slowly pushed each digit of the phone deliberately and carefully. After only two ringtones, a cheerful sounding female at the other end announced, "Grosvenor Snackfoods - may I help you?"

"Yes, please, may I speak to Herbert Grosvenor? This is Sidney Button, the CEO of Button Engineering in the U.K."

"I will just check that he is free", she responded. Then, after a short pause, a slow drawling male voice came onto the line. "Well, hello Sidney, how are you, sir?" was the greeting.

"Very well, thank you", responded Sidney. "I trust you are well?"

"Yes, still thriving, thanks. It's been a good few years since we met, but I saw your son yesterday. Is that what this is about?"

"It is," hesitated Sidney, unsure quite how to proceed. "I was disappointed to hear today that he didn't convince you to buy our conveyor system for your new factory. You have been working on the old model since 1980 when I came to see you on behalf of my Father."

"You sold us a good reliable system there, and we certainly have no complaints: it is still operating at the old factory, and we shall keep it as an emergency fallback when the new factory comes on stream. But, of course, we need the best reliable and cutting edge kit for the new place. Folks are still loving our snacks, and our export guys have been expanding us into new territories."

"I'm glad to hear it. Now I know we were up against stiff competition, but I wondered if you could tell me why we didn't get your business this time? It is always good to learn from these things, and if there is anything that we can do differently to change your mind even?" Sidney tried not to sound too desperate, but the company's future may be dependent on this deal. Unfortunately, not enough new factories were being built in the U.K., and he had hoped their new, improved system would be a clincher.

"Well, of course, as Americans, we try to support local suppliers so long as their price is competitive and system reliable. We sure weren't going to take a chance on any company without a good track record like yours. You know, when we bought from you back in the sixties, you weren't the absolute cheapest, but we could see that your gear was sturdily manufactured and more reliable than the cheaper competition. That was a good decision that I have never regretted."

"I'm delighted to hear that", assured Sidney warmly. "So, what was it that we got wrong?"

"It is a little difficult to say, my old friend, and I hope you will not hold it against me for being honest with you", replied Herbert. "Tell the truth and shame the Devil, my old Pappy used to say, and I guess that it is still valid. I had my technical whizz kid here too, and he had convinced me that we needed a system that avoided jams when one section got behind. I understand that your company has come up with something along those lines, but when we asked your boy Gerry about it, he couldn't answer our questions and seemed to fudge around the problem. I'm afraid we lost a bit of confidence there: it is a huge investment, and we have to get it right. I took over from my Pappy, and I guess he will someday do the same as your oldest. Sorry to say but we didn't take to him. He was ten minutes late for our meeting and looked like he had just dragged himself out of bed. He yawned several times and appeared to be hungover! You know that we are a family company with Christian values. None of us is perfect, but he had to show up appropriately if he wanted our business. I'm really sorry to have to tell you all that and all, but you did ask the reason why you didn't get our business. I'd hope that if ever one of my family acted like that, a friend would let me know."

"Indeed!" exclaimed Sidney in shock. "I can only apologise profusely on behalf of our company. Thank you for being candid with me. I really appreciate it. I shall, of course, be taking action on this, rest assured."

"Don't you go upsetting yourself", said Herbert. "You were not responsible, and I know you to be a good man. I have another meeting about to start, but you have a good day, and God bless" he continued terminating the conversation.

Sidney replaced the receiver and sat with his head in his hands. This was terrible news. The factory only had about two months of work in hand, with no other prospective large orders at present. They could not afford to be idle. It also appeared that Gerry had lied to him in his email, citing 'cut-throat prices' from American competition. He was returning to the U.K. today.

He turned to stare out of his office window at the adjacent industrial unit on the small estate. A forklift was loading a pallet of wine onto a lorry. They imported it through nearby Felixstowe Docks and distributed it around the U.K. He wished his company was as busy. Sighing, he added an appointment to meet Gerry at 11 am tomorrow morning when he returned to the office. He would not discuss the depressing situation with his younger brother and fellow director, Eric, until then.

Chapter 2. Felixstowe, Suffolk. Thursday, June 9th 2016.

"Can you hold all calls for me, Sheila, please? I don't want to be disturbed for the next hour or so," instructed Sidney. A minute or two later, his son Gerry knocked on the door and entered, looking a little less confident than usual. He was wearing a smart suit and tie. His mane of thick hair fell around his face, and piercing blue eyes looked out beneath it. It had to be admitted, even by other males, that he was a good looking guy. However, his Father looked up disapprovingly and nodded towards the chair on the opposite side of his desk. "Well?" Sidney enquired gruffly.

Gerry went into a well-rehearsed explanation about why they did not get the Grosvenor order, which carefully exonerated himself and placed the blame on cut-throat prices and American protectionism. Sidney listened quietly until he finished. Never let it be said that he did not hear both sides of the story. "That", he thundered, "is a pack of lies! What about turning up late with a hangover and not being able to explain the Varispeed 200 system? I have spoken with my old friend Herbert, and he told me that it was the sort of system they were looking for! It seems that you didn't even understand it."

"It's true that I don't have the technical grasp that you and Uncle Eric have", apologised Gerry. "I even spent an hour with him last week before I left, but he doesn't explain things well. He's a genius engineer, but he talks purely in technical terms, most of which I do not understand. The night before I visited, I got into a state because I knew I couldn't explain the technicalities. I could tell them what it does, joining the controls together so that different conveyors adjust for hold-ups or gaps on others in the system, but I admit that how it does it is still a mystery to me. They had another engineer there with Herbert Grosvenor tying me up in knots."

"Hmph!" snorted Sidney. "Did you never consider coming to me beforehand? You could have asked for a better explanation. You could even have even requested for myself or Eric to go with you. Your attitude has lost the order and may well lead to losing this company if another contract cannot be found quickly. This isn't the first time you have let me down, Gerry. Maybe your love of the high life doesn't fit with a plain old engineering company. Fast cars, women and drinking too much are hardly the image we want, is it?"

"No, but I .."

"Get out! Leave me to consider what needs to be done. I will have to discuss the situation with Eric – it affects the whole company."

The door slammed as Gerry left, but it was a futile gesture. He knew his future was in the balance. So instead of returning to his office, he headed for the stairs and down to his sports car in the carpark. Then, revving the engine, he blasted out onto the industrial estate road at speed.

Sidney took a few minutes to compose himself and collect his thoughts before descending the stairs himself to consult with his younger brother Eric. As usual, he was ensconced in his workshop-cum-office surrounded with diagrams on the walls, odd components from machines on the floor in piles and a desk so covered in scraps of paper that it could only be identified by its legs. Unlike Sidney, he was distinctly untidy in appearance as well: a dirty white lab coat smeared with oil and splashes of solder, worn sandals over socks and hair that fanned out in a halo. He held up his hand to Sidney to stop him speaking until he had scribbled some undecipherable note to himself. "Hello Sid, how are you today?" he asked brightly. He was the only person ever allowed to abbreviate his brother's name, a relic from their childhood together.

"Unhappy, I'm afraid", replied Sidney and gave a brief precis of what had occurred before pausing for reaction.

"Dear me", commented Eric consolingly. "It does sound as if young Gerry has overstepped the mark this time. I blame myself if he went to the States unprepared, but as you say, he is old enough to know when to know to ask for help. Hitting the booze certainly wasn't the solution."

"The trouble is, we haven't got more than a couple of months of work on the books. So I have to warn you that the whole company may be in danger. What Gloria said the other time is coming to fruition much sooner than we both expected. No new factories being built, no new mines wanting conveyors either. She said that there is so much surplus equipment around that it is being broken up for scrap rather than being re-purposed," said Sidney disconsolately.

"When father switched to making conveyor belts for the war effort, it was the making of this company", reminisced Eric. "The trouble is, we made them too good. I was talking to the chap from Warnocks the other time. He told me that our system installed in 1950 is still working well: all they do is change the belts once in a while. Excellent reputation, but it doesn't result in more business. I was hoping my Varispeed 200 control system would keep us up with demand, but it seems that it is not required in this country."

"Bless you, Eric, that system you designed is damned good. Maybe we will have to look at different products, but it is hard when this is all we have ever known. What do we do about Gerry, though?"

"You know I have always had a soft spot for him, but I must admit he is not helping our dilemma at present. However, I am no good at the 'people' stuff and never have been. I stick to what I know, which is engineering and quality control. Those lads in the factory are first class, and I would be sorry to see any of them out of a job. I will leave the decision over Gerry to you and back you up on whatever you decide. Thanks for letting me know the situation."

Seeking a little respite from his woes, Sidney opened the door into the factory at about 12:30 and wandered around, saying hello or nodding to the workers. He always thought this excellent for morale but was now wondering, 'theirs or mine?' It gave anyone a chance to speak to him if they wanted to bring up any issue informally. However, today they had just finished lunch and were all involved in the final assembly of a large conveyor together. It seemed as if everyone knew where they should be and what they should be doing, including the apprentice Michael Dooley who gave him a broad grin.

As Sidney wearily climbed the stairs to his office, he reflected that it was the decision (or lack of one) he expected from Eric. Eric preferred to stick with his speciality and let the buck stop with the M.D. Sidney's wife Kathleen would be heartbroken if he sacked her darling Gerry, but what else could he do? Maybe he would have to handle sales himself for a while: he had done the role before under his Father Edward and knew how hard it could be. He needed to think things out carefully before making any rash decisions. Father had called him 'a safe pair of hands' when he retired and made him Managing Director. Was that still the case?

It was about 3 pm when a crash followed by a piercing scream was heard on the top floor of Button Engineering. Staff came out of their offices to find a distraught Sheila. All she could say was, "Sidney is dead!"

Clive emerged first from his accounts office together with the factory manager Tim McCauley. He comforted his wife Sheila in his arms whilst Tim strode through the open door of Sidney's office. Then, just as quickly, Tim exited and shut the door. "Please don't go in there!" he said to Gloria, who had just left her marketing office. "Best get us all a cup of tea while I phone the police and ambulance." He crossed to Sheila's desk and phoned 999. "Hello, yes, I require police and an ambulance. Police yes? I believe there has been a murder. My name is Tim McCauley, and I am the Factory Manager here at Button Engineering." He gave the address and thanked the operator. Then, turning to the expectant staff, he added with a quiver in his voice, "The police says that nobody is to leave or go in that room. I'm going downstairs to tell Eric and my lads."

Conveyor Belt Corpse

Nobody said anything for a moment until Gloria burst out, "My poor Daddy! Who could do such a wicked thing? Are you sure?" Nobody answered her, but at that moment, having been alerted by Tim, Eric bounded up the stairs. He looked shaken but soon took charge:

"Obviously, it is all a terrible shock for everyone. I suggest we all have a cup of sweet tea whilst we wait for the police. Maybe you could be thinking about anybody you have seen entering the building today or any person seen acting suspiciously. The police will want to know. Is everybody here?" he asked.

Sheila responded: "Gerry went off at about noon. I haven't seen him since."

Clive added, "Oh yes, and Gordon Barker went off to collect some stationary. He should be back soon. Do you think I ought to ring Mum? Somebody ought to let her know."

"That's OK, and I will do that now," said Eric. "I was just thinking about it." He picked up the phone on Sheila's desk and called Kathleen. The others made themselves scarce to give him some privacy. By the time he got off the phone, the police had arrived. A sergeant ensured that the scene was undisturbed by putting an officer on duty at the door whilst he called his station to update them. "Nobody leaves until we say, ladies and gents, please", he repeated in each office." He went down to the factory floor with

Eric and repeated the message. Tim and the workers all sat around very subdued. Just then, the door to the factory opened, and a figure in dark blue trousers and a shirt and tie entered. "Hello lads, what's going on with all the police?" he asked cheerily.

"This is Gordon Barker," explained Tim to the Sergeant. "He was out in the van collecting some stuff." He turned to Gordon and explained the situation.

A little later, two forensics officers entered Sidney's office in white plastic coveralls and masks. Flashes of photography could be seen through the partly open doorway by Sheila as she sat back at her desk, sipping a mug of tea. She put it down and wandered over to the office of Gloria. It was neat and had boards around the wall, mainly filled with marketing leaflet layouts and graphs of sales in steep downward angles. Gloria sat hunched over her desk, quietly weeping. Sheila was unsure what to do, not having a close relationship but put a comforting hand tentatively on her shoulder. "I'm sorry, Gloria, I know how much you loved your father," she said in a low voice. She was disturbed from offering any further condolences by the sound of two more people coming up the stairs and went back to her desk to intercept them.

The older man wore a pinstripe dark blue suit and a serious expression. "Hello, I'm DCI Webb, and this is DS Newton," he said, proffering a police I.D. card. Just then, Eric appeared from the stairs and greeted them.

"Good afternoon, I'm Eric Button. I'm the dead man's brother and the other director of Button Engineering. Sheila here found him at about 3 pm, and our factory manager went in briefly to check. We have kept the room closed since then until your uniformed officers arrived."

The younger detective DS Newton thanked him before following his boss into the scene of the murder. In contrast to his boss, he wore a black leather jacket and grey needlecord trousers. His pale blue shirt was open-necked, and his hair fashionably tousled. After stepping over a broken mug and tea stain on the wooden floor, the pair surveyed the death scene: Sidney Button was stretched back in his chair, lolled over to his right side. His head was tilted backwards, eyes staring blankly upwards, and just between his collar and beard were some vivid red marks around his neck. His arms hung down, and the tongue was slightly protruding from the lips. The forensic pathologist Dr Deborah Wilson was stooping to look closely at the patterns when they entered but straightened up as she saw the detectives enter. "Good afternoon, but not for Sidney Button, it seems," she said. The other Scene of Crime officer had finished taking photos, so he left them to their discussion.

"So, is it strangulation then?" asked Webb.

"Yes, but these vertical marks are unusual – do you see them?" she asked.

"Yes, so was he throttled with something ribbed do you think?" asked Webb.

"It looks pretty likely, although I will have to check whether there are any other more injuries when I get him back to the lab", replied Dr Wilson. "It looks as though there are petechiae present in the eyes – sorry, red spots often associated with asphyxiation.

Anxious to be involved (especially when the attractive Doctor was involved) DS Newton made a suggestion: "I think they make conveyor machinery here. Could it be a toothed belt, do you think?"

"Yes, that is a good possibility, but it would have to be quite a narrow one – about 100mm at the most judging from the width of the strangulation marks. I haven't spotted anything that would fit the bill, but of course, you will have to check. As for timing, the nearest I can say is this afternoon at present. The Sergeant mentioned that he had been seen at around just after lunchtime, and it was called in just after 3 o'clock, so, not too wider a time frame for you."

"Thank you very much, Doctor Wilson", concluded Webb. "I will let you finish up here and look forward to seeing your report.

Conveyor Belt Corpse

"Cheers!" added DS Newton, smiling back at her as they exited to find the uniformed Sergeant waiting for them discreetly at the top of the stairs, together with Eric Button.

"Hello, sirs", he greeted them. I have all the factory hands detained downstairs. We have taken statements from them, and they all claim not to have left the shopfloor or come upstairs today, apart from the manager. Shall we let them go – they were all working together, so they corroborated each other's stories?"

"Yes, you may as well, so long as you have all their details. Send the manager upstairs to join the rest of his colleagues, though, please, if you will," instructed Webb. "Oh, and I'm guessing this place will be off-limits tomorrow, so let them know not to come into work tomorrow. Sorry Mr Button, but we will need to make a thorough search of the entire premises. Do you employ a cleaner?"

"Yes, they come in on Tuesday and Thursday nights. Do you want me to put them off?" asked Eric.

"That would be great if you could, Mr Button. I want as little disturbance to the crime scene as possible until we are finished," added Webb. Then, seeing the other SOCO officer standing there, he addressed him as well: "Can you bag up the victim's laptop and get it analysed for emails over the last 30 days. There was a notepad on the desk as well. Maybe you can take that away too – I think it had something written on it."

"Yes, sir, I will do. I have already taken a picture of it" He clicked the controls of his camera to bring a shot onscreen. "Looks like it says 'G.B?' he said. I'll see if it has any impressions from the previous page."

"Good man!" praised Webb. Then, after everyone else had gone, he turned to Newton and asked, "Did you spot it as well?" With a grin, Newton turned his notebook over, showing the same G.B? message.

"OK, smartypants, why will 'His Lordship' want us to take extra diligence with this case?"

"Doesn't he always? Why should this one be any different?" queried Newton.

"You didn't notice the ring on the little finger of his right hand? It was Masonic – the old square and compasses badge. We have to look after his Brothers! Even if the Police are expected to declare their membership nowadays, there's still too much of an 'old boy' network for my liking. You are not 'on the square' yourself, Newton, I suppose?"

"Never been asked, and doubt whether I'd accept", retorted Newton. "I wouldn't fancy being in any club that included 'His Lordship' as a member."

Webb grinned. 'His Lordship' was how he referred to his boss Detective Superintendent Hardy. He disliked him and never referred to him by name unless he could help it, on the basis that officers may forget him when he was gone. Nevertheless, he was glad that the name was catching on with his squad. "Right, we'd better get some preliminary interviews done. I will take the brother Eric and the factory manager. Maybe you can start on the others, DS Newton, and we'll see where we have got. We'd better let them go when we have seen each of them. Before you do, though, ring the team and tell them that I want them to be in the office before 8 am tomorrow for a briefing and distribution of tasks."

"No problem, sir," assured Newton.

Chapter 3

As Sheila Button was still at her reception desk as he walked through the door to the offices, Colin Newton decided to start with her:

"I work as a secretary for the company, and I am married to Clive Button. He is the youngest son of Sidney Button and manages the accounts. The rest make their drinks, but I take one into the M.D at 10:30 & 3 pm each day. This afternoon I knocked and entered as usual, and that's when I found him! (She paused to dab her eyes with a screwed up tissue.) I dropped the mug of tea I was carrying and ran out, screaming for help. My husband and Tim, the factory manager, arrived first. I was in such a state that Tim McCauley went in while my Clive stayed with me. Then Tim came out again and phoned the police."

"Perfect, Mrs Button", reassured Newton. "Now, from your desk, you can see everyone coming and going on the 1st floor. Did you see anyone go in or out in the afternoon?

"Gordon Barker went out on an errand at about 12:30. Tim McCauley came up to visit Clive at about two, but apart from that, no. Most of them eat lunch at their desks – there is nowhere much to go on this industrial estate. The door to the stairs was closed because it is a fire door., so I did not see if anyone came up or down the stairs to see Sidney without coming in here. I'm not at my desk all the time: sometimes I need to use the photocopier at the other end or go into the stationery cupboard, loo or kitchen. I also sort the post in the morning and distribute it, then collect, frank and take the outgoing mail to the postbox along the road in the afternoon. All the offices have direct telephone lines, so it doesn't matter if I am away from my desk for a short while."

There was a pause whilst Newton finished writing his notes. "Is there anything else I should know?" he asked.

"Well," Sheila said hesitantly. "This morning, my Father-in-law Sidney had an appointment with his oldest son Gerry at 11 and asked not to be disturbed. Gerry has just come back from a sales trip in America. Then, at about 12, I heard raised voices and a slammed door in the corridor outside. Gerry must have left because he didn't come back in here. I haven't seen him since."

"Do you know what they were arguing about?" asked Newton.

"No, I couldn't hear clearly", explained Sheila.

"We, thank you for all that", said Newton. "My boss should be talking to your husband at present, but then you are both free to leave. Who uses that office there?"

"That is Gloria Button, Sidney's daughter. She does all our marketing and the website."

Newton knocked on the door and heard a faint 'come in' before entering. Gloria was an attractive blonde woman, probably in her mid-twenties, but her mascara had run, and her eyes were puffy with tears. She wore a pink blouse and a short leather skirt which revealed a long pair of legs much to Newton's liking. She gestured to a seat, and Newton sat down beside a drawing board with artwork for machinery fixed to it. "I am sorry for the loss of your father, but I need to ask a few questions, and then you can go", commenced Newton. Can I start by asking when you last saw your Father please?"

"At breakfast this morning", Gloria replied huskily. "I travelled separately because I intended to go out straight from work. Sometimes I share a ride in Daddy's Bentley – I still live, sorry did live, at home with him and my Mother. So when I got here, I got straight to work designing some website changes for the new system. It takes a lot of concentration. So other than popping out to make a cup of tea, I have been in here all day until I heard the commotion."

"Did you get on well with your father, Miss Button?" Newton queried.

"Oh yes, he was a sweety. He could be a bit protective, especially towards any new boyfriend I may have brought home, but his bark was worse than his bite. Mummy once said that when he talked to potential suitors, he grilled them like cheese!" She gave a weak laugh, and Newton joined in with a chuckle.

"What about the rest of the family?" asked Newton, hoping that an open question may elicit some unguarded gossip.

"Well, there is my brother Clive the accountant. He's a bit of a stick-in-the-mud but gets livened up a bit by his wife, Sheila. She worked here for two years before they went out together. I wouldn't be surprised if she didn't ask him out! She is still here as a secretary. Then there is my older brother Gerry who handles sales. He is a bit of a free spirit, and I don't think it suits him, but of course, Daddy wanted to groom him to take over eventually. He lives at a flat in town so that he can come and go as he pleases without Daddys disapproval.

My Grandfather Edward Button started the company and handed it on to Daddy, his oldest son. His youngest brother, my uncle Eric trained as an engineer. He is a sweet man but seems to live in a world of his own down there in his workshop. As for me, I have been applying to move on: I think I am pretty capable of doing more than marketing for a small family company with a limited future, but it has given me some experience. I guess I will have to put that on hold for a while now: I wouldn't leave them in the lurch at a time like this, and Mummy will need me to live at home now for a bit longer, I think."

"I'm guessing that you will want to get home to her now", offered Newton sympathetically. He noticed she was not wearing an engagement ring and regretted the golden rule of not forming relationships connected to a case. It would be likely that comforting and consoling would be required, but unfortunately, he had to rule himself out. "Is there anything else I should know? Did your Father have any enemies?" he asked.

"Oh no! His biggest enemy has been lack of orders, as you can see from the charts," she responded, indicating the coloured computer graphics on the wall. "I'm afraid that we are not big enough to attract the attention of any serious rivals, and other than his Masonic Lodge, Daddy had few contacts outside of the family."

"OK, thank you very much, that has all been most helpful. Now I suggest you get off home to your Mother, but be careful how you go. Is it far?" Newton asked.

"No, just on the outskirts of Kirton," she replied. "Thank you for listening to me ramble on."

"Not at all", replied Newton. "It's what policemen do," He opened the door for Gloria and followed her out just as Ron Webb exited another door further along the corridor. They caught up with each other on who had been seen. Ron had interviewed Eric and Tim, so that left Gordon Barker and Clive Button. "I'd most like to see the son Gerry who stormed off this morning. Eric had been trying to raise him on his mobile phone, but it is switched off. I have his home address, so we may have to go there later if he has returned home. Just then, the uniformed Sergeant appeared.

"Ah, just the man!" exclaimed Webb. "Do you think that you could get an officer to go to this address in Felixstowe and check if Gerry Button is at home, please? If he is, keep him there and let us know. I have also got his car registration: it's a red Mazda MX5 sports car. Can you put out a call to watch out for it as well?"

"Of course, sir – right away", responded the Sergeant and went off. Webb updated his colleague:

"The factory manager Tim McCauley says he was in a meeting with Clive Button in the accounts office all afternoon. Clive says the same, so they give each other alibi's or are both lying. They also reckoned that Barker chap went off on an errand in the van once he had finished his lunch with the factory lads at about 12:30. Sidney walked onto the shop floor just after that, which was the last time he was seen alive. I suppose Barker or Gerry could have hung around to do the murder before they left? Barker could even have gone and hidden in Eric Buttons office. He wasn't back until after the body was discovered, and the Sergeant and the factory hands all said he seemed unaware of what had happened until they told him."

"OK, shall I check him out while you talk to Eric, sir?" offered Newton.

"Yes, it shouldn't take too long", replied Webb.

As he sat opposite Gordon Barker in the empty sales office, Newton thought he detected signs of nervousness: a sweaty forehead despite the coolness of the office and a foot-tapping against the floor. Of course, most ordinary people are nervous about being interviewed by the police, however honest and innocent they are, but Newton's professional radar was switched on to the signs. "So what do you actually do for Button Engineering, Mr Barker?" he asked.

"Well, to be honest, anything required", responded Gordon. "I'm partly paid by the Button family, partly by the company. I act, sorry, acted as chauffeur to Sidney Button and occasionally to other family members. I also do some gardening and general household repairs for them – like fixing a shelf or unblocking a sink. The rest of my time I work here, making deliveries of the smaller equipment, collecting stuff, general maintenance and cleaning and so on."

"Ah good, that explains things," said Newton trying to lull him into a sense of security. "So what did you work at today then? I understand you didn't arrive back here until after the death of Sidney Button?"

"Yes, that's right. It was a bit embarrassing, really: I bounced into the factory all cheery like, not knowing what had happened until they told me. Anyway, I started the day by chauffeuring Mr Button into work from his home in Kirton. He had a heart condition so that he couldn't drive. His daughter Gloria travelled separately in her Mini because she said she was going out straight from work into Felixstowe. I adjusted a ballcock on a toilet downstairs and replaced a washer on a dripping tap the rest of the morning. Then I had my sandwiches with the lads before going off in the van to fetch some stationary from Warnocks. It was ready yesterday, but the van was in for its MOT and service at the garage on the industrial estate, so they got me to do it this afternoon. I planned to have a cup of tea when I returned before driving Mr Button home," he concluded chattily. "Terrible business; he was a nice boss."

"You must have got to know him more than most people here", commented Newton. "Did he seem anxious about anything lately or upset anyone?"

"He was pleasant but not very talkative in the car. He usually read his newspaper on the way here in the morning and often seemed lost in thought on the way home, so we didn't often talk much. He didn't have anybody that hated him enough to kill him, I wouldn't think. It's a family firm, so they tend to sort out differences by talking directly rather than boardroom battles. I guess they have disputes like any family, and I know that he didn't always see eye to eye with Gerry. Gloria still lives at home, but Gerry Button has a flat in the Old Town of Felixstowe, and Clive Button lives with his wife Sheila on the Trinity Estate, the other side of town. Fortunately, I live not far from Sidney and his wife Kathleen in Kirton."

"Well, thank you for that, Mr Barker," said Newton, closing his notebook "unless there is anything else you can tell me, you may as well get back to Kirton yourself."

"Thank you, sir!" said Gordon sounding a little relieved. "I shall take the Bentley back in case the family need it tomorrow, and I'd rather not leave it here."

Webb had been interviewing Eric Button in his workshop in the meantime. He was getting an initial description from him of what happened:

"Yes, so I wasn't aware of anything happening until Tim knocked on my door. It was closed, and I had some machinery running, so I hadn't heard a thing," he was explaining. "As the only other director, I sort of took charge from then, but Tim had already rung 999. I suppose I must mention that there had been a problem in the morning, which was the last time I saw my brother Sid. He had been talking with Gerry, my nephew that handles sales. It seems that he had made a bit of a cock-up in the States, and he was considering firing him. As you probably gathered, it is a family firm, and as such, the business and family issues sometimes get mixed together. Sid has never really forgiven Gerry for something that happened when he was at school years ago. He got expelled without doing his exams, and consequently, Sid pushed him into working here, where I think he thought he could keep an eye on him. It hasn't really worked, in my opinion. Gerry has a bit of a spark to him, but not having any qualifications didn't have much choice at the time. I am surprised he hasn't left of his own accord before now. Sid came and told me about it at about 12. As he is Gerry's Father, I could not ask him to fire his son – it wouldn't be right. So he had to decide for himself, as the Managing Director for the good of the company. That was the last time I saw him. I have been in my workroom ever since, trying to write a new technical specification for a piece of kit we have modified, and running a stress test on a new sort of belt."

"Talking of belts," Webb interjected before Eric wandered further off the point ", do you have belts that are no wider than 100mm in the building that are toothed?"

"Oh yes, there are quite a few around. Look!" he said, ferreting into a box of mixed materials on the floor. "Here's a piece of one. They are usually of a 2 - metre length, but I have cut this one for an experiment. We use them on our Boxer 100 machine, which is mainly for moving cartons a short distance between machines on a production line. As these are small, they are handy to send out as samples with brochure requests, although we buy them in a thousand at a time from another supplier."

"May I keep this piece, please?" asked Webb. "There is a possibility that it was something like this that was used to strangle your brother."

"Oh, dear! That would suggest someone from within," said Eric in horror. "Although you can find them in the factory, this office and the stationary room. I know that they had a falling out, but I find it hard to believe that it was Gerry, even if he has disappeared. He would have been upset, but he has never struck me as being violent. Foolish sometimes, but I like the chap, actually – he makes me laugh. I still haven't managed to get him to answer his phone – it sounds like it is switched off."

"Well, sir, we have no firm ideas at the moment, but we would like to speak to him, of course. Have you any idea of anyone falling out with your brother? Any disgruntled ex-employees?" queried Webb.

"No, you can rule that out. We are lucky to have a very stable workforce here. The last one to join was young Michael Dooley, the apprentice. That must have been nearly three years ago because he qualifies as an engineer soon. He replaced a chap called Billy Sullivan, who retired at 65. That was the last person to leave, three years ago. I cannot think of anyone else that would even dislike my brother, let alone want to murder him. This situation is shocking, and I don't know what to think or do at the moment."

"Well, thank you very much, Mr Button. As I said, we will need to be in here tomorrow, and inevitably I will have more questions later. So I will have a man on duty here for tonight, which will save you returning early in the morning to let us in again."

"Thank you very much," replied Eric. "Is there anything else I can help you with?"

"Since we will be searching the whole building, is it possible to have any keys required, please?" Webb requested.

"Certainly!" responded Eric. "There is a full set of keys on hooks inside the office next door belonging to Tim McCauley, the factory manager. If I just check that he has left his door open, you can use any of those, but please replace them." Webb followed him out into the corridor. Eric tried the adjoining door, and it opened. "Just there", he pointed, indicating the row of hooks. "I'll be off then if there is nothing else?" he said. As Webb shook his head, Eric added, "I do hope young Gerry is OK. He can be a chump, as I told you earlier, but I cannot believe he would have harmed his Father!" he said. I'll just grab my coat and switch off the machinery in my room."

Gordon Barker was also leaving. He made his way past Webb and Eric in the corridor with a nod. Newton, who had stayed behind in the sales office to finish writing up his notes, descended the stairs a few minutes later. As he got to the front door, he could see Webb talking on his mobile phone in front of the building. A minute or two later, Gordon Barker re-emerged in the Bentley and exited the gates. Then a police patrol car entered and parked up by the front entrance close to where Newton and Webb were standing. Webb finished his call and talked to the uniformed Constable emerging from the patrol car. "Nobody in or out except for police. That especially includes employees since we haven't found the murder weapon yet. Sit in your car by all means, but stay alert, Constable!" he instructed.

Turning to Newton, he nodded to him to accompany him back into the building. He knocked on the door marked 'Research & Development', and Eric Button opened it. "That is the last employee gone", informed Webb. "I have just now had a call to say that your nephew Gerry is now at his flat, so we are about to go and see him there. We have one of our men on the door, so you can leave it unlocked with the alarm off.

Just then, there was a rattle from the cat flap at the end of the corridor, and a large tortoiseshell cat strutted in. "Good evening Brunel" called Eric. The cat slowly made its way to him and purred, rubbing herself against his legs. "There can't be many companies that employ the famous Brunel," he said, bending to stroke him. "He was an excellent engineer, but this one is a fantastic mouser. Soon sorted out our problem a year or two back, and not a mouse has dared to show itself since. He has the run of the place and comes and goes as he pleases." He looked towards the gap under the stairs where two bowls and a litter tray lay. "Yes, Sheila has left you some food out; you will not starve until we return," he added, addressing the cat.

The detectives watched Eric depart, head bowed and a grim expression on his face. When he had left, Webb told Newton that he had not gained much from his interview with Eric that they did not know already, other than the cause of Gerry rushing off earlier in the day.

"From what I've learnt, he may not have much of a company to take over", commented Newton. "I will explain in the car on the way to Gerry's" They walked along the corridor to the backdoor and a grubby window overlooking the rough carpark behind the building, beyond the stairs.

The door had the catflap. Newton checked that the door was locked and peered out. "Some cats are real killers, but I don't think we can put Brunel in the frame here. Only your car and the company van in the carpark", he commented. "I'd like to take a quick look at that before we leave," he said, almost to himself. Webb did not query this: if an officer had a notion, it was often better to let them act upon it. Who knew what it might lead to?

Having waved to the sentinel Constable out front in his car, the pair walked around the back to the carpark. Newton tried the backdoor of the long Mercedes van, but it was locked. The driver and passenger doors were also secured, but he peered in through the window anyway. Then, seemingly satisfied, he joined Webb in his Rover, and they made their way to Gerry Button's flat, with Newton filling Webb I on what he had found out along the way.

Chapter 4.

Having abstained from his habit for the duration of their visit, Webb leant over to extract a mint humbug from the bag in his car. Newton was known not to partake, so he didn't bother to offer him one. The June sun was now low in the sky, and they both tilted the sun visors to avoid the glare of it sparkling from the sea as they approached the address given for Gerry Button's flat. It was situated in an old hotel that had been converted to an apartment building. DS Colin Newton spotted the red Mazda MX5 sports car belonging to Gerry a few spaces further along the carpark as they parked.

"Nice but no cigar", commented DCI Webb. "From the numbering, his flat is at the back without a sea view, so a bit less expensive." A cramped lift took them to the second floor, and Colin pushed the doorbell. Not hearing any chimes, he knocked on the door with his fist instead, just before it opened. "Alright, give me a chance to answer it!" was the annoyed greeting from a dishevelled looking man of about 30. The pair of detectives held up their warrant cards. "I am DCI Webb, and this is my colleague DS Newton" announced Ron. "Are you Mr Button? May we come in?"

"Yes, I was told to expect someone," said Gerry turning and speaking over his shoulder as he walked back into the room. They followed him,

Newton closing the door behind him. After they were all seated, DCI Webb did the formal bit of condolences for his loss. "Yes, the uniformed officer told me the old man was dead but don't expect me to cry crocodile tears. I have had enough of him, the pompous old dinosaur. Was it his heart?"

"Ah, it appears that you were not told earlier. I'm sorry to say that your father was murdered. When did you last see him?" asked Webb. By now, Newton was busily writing into his notebook, trying to get down what was being said.

"We had a meeting at 11 this morning. Unfortunately, it did not go well, and I left about an hour later. I cannot be sure of the time as I was too upset." Gerry pulled a cigarette out and lit it. There were many stubs in an ashtray, a half-empty whiskey bottle, and a glass tumbler on the table. By the smell of him, Gerry had been using both heavily, and some ash had fallen onto his trouser leg. His shirt collar was open, and a tie pulled to one side, hanging still knotted.

"Where did you go when you left your father's office Mr Button?" asked Webb.

"What is this? Are you trying to get me to give you some sort of alibi? I might not like him much, but I am his son!" retorted Gerry angrily. "You should be out finding his killer!"

"We had to ask everybody from the company where they were, and it is part of the process. We spoke to them all this afternoon, so it just leaves you. Did you go back to the office? Or if not, where did you go?"

Sighing, Gerry muttered, "I drove to the coast near Bawdsey Ferry and sat looking out to sea. It is peaceful there, and I needed to think. Before you ask, no, I didn't see anyone else there to talk to. If you have been talking to the others at the company, they will have no doubt been filling you in. All smiling faces but ready with the stab in the back. I failed to get a vital order in America. My job is on the line. I never wanted to work there, but I got bullied into it by Dad. I'm not cut out to understand engineering, and what they do is stuck in the past, but they can't see it because it is all they have ever done. They may as well be manufacturing gas lamps!" His tone was now angry, and his face, initially pale, was now flushed with colour. His blue eyes flashed as they looked up from under a thick fringe of black hair.

Seeing a chance to contribute, Newton glanced over at Webb, who gave him a discreet nod. Then, adopting a conciliatory tone, Colin Newton posed a question:

"I can understand you are upset, but why would you say that the others are against you, that they would 'stab you in the back? I'm trying to understand here, and it is only fair that you tell your side of the story."

"Yeah, well, my brother Clive went off and got qualified as an accountant. Safe, reliable old Clive, a real golden boy, but it is all he knows, and I think he is jealous of me gadding around on an expense account that he scrutinises like Scrooge. His wife Sheila smiles sweetly, but I believe she is very ambitious for him, so she loves to see me fail. It gives him a better chance of taking over the company from Dad.

My sister Gloria is a real Daddy's Girl and can do no wrong according to him and Mother, but that's not what I hear around the bars of Felixstowe! I overheard her talking to a London recruitment agency the other time, so they may get a shock when she ups and goes. I don't think anyone else knows. Uncle Eric is alright, I suppose in his 'mad professor' sort of way, but he has always left the decisions to Dad, although he has 45% of the shares.

Nobody builds factories in the U.K. anymore, and it will be worse still if the country votes to leave the E.C. later this year. I have tried to tell them to get into something else, but they will not listen. Other countries have their own manufacturers of conveyors, so why pay to import ours? I feel sorry for the lads on the shop floor. They produce reliable machinery, but if they become redundant, the only significant employer around here is Felixstowe Docks, and I cannot see them wanting many engineers. You'd think Tim McCauley would put in a word – everyone trusts him, but he seems too close to 'Cautious Clive' the counter of beans."

"So who do you think may have killed your father then?" asked Webb.

"Well, anyone can walk in to through the front door from 8 am when Tim arrives and unlocks it. I don't think either his door on the left or Uncle Erics just past it has windows, so they would not hear or see anyone. If you take the factory door to the right, one of the engineers would see you and ask what you were doing. They don't like strangers wandering around because there is dangerous machinery in there. However, you could walk past their door, which is always closed and go straight up the stairs. It would be easy to get to Dads office along the corridor without being seen by 'Snoopy Sheila.' She sits at the entrance to the suite of offices but keeps the fire door closed. She wouldn't see anyone unless someone else was going through the door."

"What about staff from the suite of offices?" asked Newton.

"Sheila would see them go past her if she was there but isn't always at her desk. Mind you, she gets pretty annoyed if you go straight to your office without her seeing you. She wants to know everything that is going on and where everybody is. Sheila thinks she is in charge sometimes, but she most definitely is not!" said Gerry emphatically.

"What about enemies?" continued Webb. "Anyone fallen out with your father?"

"Only me and I did not kill him. He is in the Masons, but I don't know who any of them are. He is too dull to be a threat to anyone, really, and doesn't have many friends. I have no idea, I'm afraid."

"Who might benefit from his death, do you think? Do you know anything about his will?" asked Webb.

"Everything goes to Mum: the house, car, savings and company shares. Dad owned 55%, but at the rate we are going, they will not be worth much," was the reply. "I really ought to ring Mum – she will be in a state."

"We'll leave you to do that, Mr Button," said Webb. "Thank you for your time. The factory will be closed tomorrow so that our chaps can search it. So goodbye, we'll be in touch."

As the pair of detectives drove back to the police H.Q. at Martlesham, Newton commented, "He didn't seem very upset at the death of his father, or even surprised. It was interesting that he never mentioned Gordon Barker when he was criticising everyone. Either he doesn't consider him an essential part of the company, or he didn't want to talk about him."

Webb smiled. "Very good! I was thinking the same. Maybe you had better check out this Gordon tomorrow."

Chapter 5. Friday, June 10th 2016.

The Serious Crime Squad (also known sometimes as the Murder Squad) were all assembled early in the Suffolk Police H.Q. squad room in Martlesham, just outside Ipswich. The newest member, DC Chris Winter, who had only joined them nine months ago, got the rookies' job of setting up the incident whiteboard, with what little they knew so far. He headed it with yesterdays date and the name Sidney Button, plus a location of Button Engineering, Felixstowe. He would have to add details as they emerged from DCI Webb and DS Newton.

DC Will Catesby looked eager to get started and twiddled a pen whilst supping a mug of tea. He had made it, plus other drinks for DC Peggy Catchpole and Chris. Peggy was on her computer finding out what she could about Button Engineering. It would inevitably be asked for, and she liked to impress by being ahead of what her bosses wanted. She was both intelligent and ambitious and married to a cop in Traffic Division.

DS Colin Newton arrived just before DCI Ron Webb. "If you can make me a cuppa, I can add quite a bit to your board," he offered.

"Make that two please", boomed Webb as he walked to the front of the group and perched himself on the edge of a table. From his higher position, he had a clear view of all his team, and as an afterthought, bid them 'Good Morning.' He gave Chris a chance to finish making the tea and took a couple of sips before launching a briefing of what had been found out yesterday. From time to time, Colin added details to the narrative.

"So, we believe that Sidney was killed sometime between 1-3 pm, strangled with a small conveyor belt. It looked as though it had been done from behind as he sat in his chair, judging by the fact that the deepest marks were to the front of his throat. We should know more when we get the pathologist's post mortem report. This leads me to an important factor: SOCO did not find any weapon at the scene, and we need it! Badly!" he emphasised. "It is a fair-sized place, which will be unoccupied and open for us to search today. I am using all of you because I understand that all of the SOCO teams have been called over to a big search around Weybread, near Diss. I want you all there at Felixstowe, at least initially. As well as the belt, which may have beard hairs, saliva, blood or even fingerprints on it you should look out for anything else which may be connected. Gloves would be the obvious one since our dear friends on T.V. point out that they are essential fashion items for even the lowliest criminal."

"SOCO already has the victims laptop and notepad, but any other useful information we can obtain is to be collected and bagged", added Colin. "It could well be someone who works there, so search any desks, lockers, filing cabinets etc."

"Good point," commented Ron. "Now everyone there has given us an alibi as to where they were, some of which have yet to be validated. DC Winter, can I task you with making a sketch map of both the ground and top floors, please? Take some flip chart sheets and markers so we can have something to relate their details to."

"Yes, sir!" acknowledged Winter. Webb consulted some notes he had made in his pocketbook and allotted tasks:

"DS Newton to major on the research lab – I know it is a mess, so you are going to have to take time and be methodical. I will cover the M.D.s office. DC Catchpole, you start upstairs in the Marketing Office and then move onto Accounts next door. D.C. Catesby start with the kitchen, toilets and stationary room upstairs. Whoever finishes first have a thorough search of the sales office – Gerry is an obvious suspect. After making your floor plans, DC Winter had better search around the secretary's desk and filing cabinets upstairs. When we have covered upstairs, we will need to search outside and through the factory. Oh, I nearly forgot: the sort of belt we are looking for is no more than 100 mm wide and about 2 metres (or about 4 inches by six and a half feet in English) long in a continuous loop but may have been cut. It has teeth on the inside. Here is a small section of one." He pulled the sample he had got from Eric from his pocket and passed it to the team to examine. "That doesn't rule out something else being used, so query anything suspicious, especially if it seems hidden. If in doubt, ask DS Newton or me. Make sure you all take plenty of gloves and wear them and enough evidence bags. Any questions?"

After shaking of heads, Webb suggested that Winter travelled with Newton, with Catesby and Catchpole with himself. It was only about twelve miles, but the heavy traffic heading for Felixstowe Docks slowed the journey to about half an hour. However, there had been a change of uniformed policeman at 6 am, and Webb told the new P.C. that he was free to go. The team split up once Webb had retrieved the keys for them.

Colin looked at the piles of papers and parts that filled Eric's workshop and scratched his head. Then he decided that he would check each piece and pile it up outside the door to avoid moving materials multiple times. It proved to be a good plan, but trying to decipher Eric's writing on scraps of paper proved more of a challenge. After an hour, he was amused to find a Xmas shopping list amongst a pile of technical data, which was the only bright spot in a laborious task. He was by now sweaty and grubby from the accumulated detritus. However, he had found nothing that suggested murder and plenty to suggest that the occupant lived up to his 'mad professor' image.

Colin had thrown the Xmas list onto the pile of stuff he had inspected, but then he picked it up again. Gloria and Sheila had been bracketed together with the word 'perfume.' Gerry, Clive and Sidney had been allocated 'wallets', but it was Kathleen's name that had caught his eye as he tossed it down. The word brooch was written beside her name, and a tiny heart had been drawn. It looked as if she might have got a more elaborate, individual gift than the rest of her relatives. Did the small heart signify that Eric was in love with his brother's wife as well? He bagged the piece of paper and found nothing else of interest, so he started to move the piles of materials back into the workshop, thinking that he had probably destroyed a unique filing system. There had been a few sections of conveyor belt, but all far too wide to have been used to strangle anyone.

Upstairs at the murder scene, Webb had bagged up the broken mug on the floor, just in case it was needed but otherwise found an office of neatness and system. There was no diary, so he suspected that Sidney maintained one on his P.C. If he didn't, it may mean that the murderer had removed it. There were neatly labelled folders and lever arch files, none of which seemed to contain much of interest, and most of which seemed to stop in the late 1970s. It looks as though most of the companies records had been computerised after the founder Edward Button had retired in around 1980. The desk produced a fine array of pens, an unopened bottle of whisky with a label saying 'Happy Xmas from all at Warnocks Printers.' It suggested to Webb that Sidney was not a secret alcoholic if he could still have an unopened bottle of scotch on his desk from Xmas until June. He looked in distaste at the well-known blended brand label: it had to be a single malt to tempt his palate. The only file of any interest was for personnel.

Along with their start dates and salaries, there were some pencilled notes that Sidney had not intended for other eyes since he had placed it into a locked desk draw. Webb put it into a bag to take back for detailed reading. Other than that, there was a plastic lunchbox containing an empty juice carton and breadcrumbs. Unless it were from another day, it would be fair to assume that Sidney had eaten his lunch yesterday before being murdered. It also explained something that had puzzled him. Sheila had said that she took him tea every day in the morning and afternoon. Presumably, he didn't require tea at lunchtime because he had a small carton of juice instead. He wrote a couple of notes in his pocketbook and left the room to see how Newton was doing downstairs. As he reached the bottom of the stairs, the door opened at the top. DC Peggy Catchpole raced down two at a time with a triumphant look on her face. She had something contained in an evidence bag.

"Whoa! there DC Catchpole," Webb said. "I applaud you for your enthusiasm but don't break your neck until you have told me what you have found!" Peggy slowed down and, catching her breath, said, "I found this in Gloria Button's desk. There was a locked drawer, but I found the key in a pencil pot. It had various ladies personal items, plus a plastic packet of four marker pens. It seemed a curious thing to keep locked up unless there is rampant theft in the office. Anyway, this little bag was tucked in the packet, hidden behind the marker pens. It has white powder in it that I wouldn't mind betting is cocaine."

"Well done, DC Catchpole!" congratulated Webb. "I don't know whether it is part of the murder plot, but it will give us more leverage to get the truth out of young miss Gloria. Excellent – see that it goes back to get tested."

"Yes, sir!" beamed Peggy. "The desk was the last place I searched, and there didn't seem anything else of interest, except sales graphs pointing rapidly downwards. So I will move on to the accounts office next door now if that is OK?"

"Certainly", responded Webb, stepping over the remaining piles of stuff from the workshop. DS

Newton stepped out into the corridor to fetch another stack of papers back. "Any luck there, DS Newton?" he queried.

"No sir, not much, although there is something that I will show you later on. It is probably unimportant."

"Very well", replied Webb, "but sometimes the smallest clue helps when we have nothing else."

"Indeed," replied Newton. "The key to the van is on the hook in the factory managers office. When I have finished here, I want to take a look inside. It may be nothing, but there has been something bothering me while I have been doing this, so I will check it out, then check search in the factory managers office as well."

"Good, follow your nose, that's the way", encouraged Webb as he continued up the stairs. It had sometimes been niggling thoughts that had previously provided results for himself, so he always encouraged this in his officers. As he entered the office suite, DC Winter looked up from the bottom draw of a filing cabinet he was searching.

"Hello sir, nothing too incriminating here other than a concealed stash of Jaffa Cakes in the secretaries desk," he joked.

"Well, I'm suspicious of anyone who doesn't like them, so she's probably in the clear! Maybe you can help D.C. Catesby now. I see that you have done the floor plans – good man!" encouraged Webb. He walked over to the kitchen area. Catesby was just emerging from one of the pair of toilets next door.

"I have checked all of the kitchen cupboards, and they are clear, including any open packets. The fridge only has milk in it. I have just checked in the cisterns of the toilets, but there is nothing there either, sir," reported Catesby.

"OK, thanks, move on to the sales office with Winter here now then," instructed Webb. "Take that place apart – Gerry Button has to be our chief suspect for the moment, and it is his office." He walked past them and entered the stationery store at the corner of the building. There was an open packet of large size latex gloves on a shelf. It was three-quarters full. Ron poked around in it to find out if any had been stuffed back in the box, but they all seemed clean and unused.

Most of the cupboard shelves were full of paper: brochures, headed notepaper, blank timesheets and the like. However, a torn open box was half full of belts on the floor, precisely the type they were looking for. The carton was labelled 100 mm x 2 metres, and a manufacturer named Nastva Ltd. Ron pulled the top one out and examined it closely in his gloved hands. Each belt had a paper sleeve holding the belt together in the middle. He ripped off the sleeve from the one he was examining. There were no marks or hairs upon it, but he did notice a serial number inside and the letters C.E. It was quite stiff in the hand, and he could hold it out horizontally from one end.

Ron considered that to be an effective, weapon the sleeve would need to be off and the belt cut through. It might be possible to use it intact, but it would then only be a metre long, and the teeth would be unlikely to come into contact with the neck. He judged that it could be done with a strong pair of scissors. He thought it would be too big and inflexible to fit into a pocket or handbag to smuggle out of the factory, even if it was cut. The only way would be to conceal it beneath the clothing, but most people only wore shirts or blouses in the warm weather, which wasn't very practical. During a night spent partly awake, he had been concerned that the killer could have already removed the murder weapon, but it seemed less likely now. He had checked, and the windows upstairs could not be opened, so there was no chance of the item being thrown out onto the car park or street. He kept the belt and label for reference in case it should be required for reference later on.

Webb started pulling each box or pile of paper out from the shelves in increasing frustration in case something had been hidden behind them. But, unfortunately, all that he found were a couple of spiders that he let escape back to their hidey holes. Giving up, at last, he exited the room to find DC Catchpole doing the same from the accounts office. She shook her head, indicating that she had not located anything else of interest. "Never mind," consoled Webb."I never had Clive down as a drug fiend anyway!" Hearing voices, Catesby and Winter emerged from the sales office. "No luck, sir," commented Catesby.

"Oh well, we have been at it all morning, so I think it's time we had a short break before tackling the factory. I spotted a burger van on the industrial estate road out of the window earlier." He took out his wallet and pulled out some banknotes. He gave it to Winter. Go with these other two and get us a burger each plus a cup of tea. No onions in my burger. Give Newton a shout on your way past and ask what he wants – they may do a lettuce leaf for him, so long as it is no too fattening!" Newton was well known for being on a permanent health kick of gyms and diets, which Webb despised after years of eating whatever was available.

When they had all gathered together again in the kitchen area, Newton (between bites of a cheese sandwich on brown bread) addressed them:

"In the Factory Manager's office, I found the MOT certificate for the van that Barker was using yesterday. It shows that the van was MOT'd on Tuesday, June 7th, as we had previously been told, at Brackenbury Motors. That garage is on this industrial estate, a few hundred yards down the road from here. Like all MOT's it shows the mileage on the day, which was 56,347 miles (he said checking the document in his hands.) So it would only have done a few hundred yards to get it back here.

Yesterday we were told that Barker left here in the van at about 12:30 when he and the factory hands finished their sandwiches. He collected some stationary from a company called Warnocks. I have been busy on my phone. Warnock's is in Trimley St. Martin, just off the High Street, only 2.8 miles away. At that time of day, I'm guessing it wouldn't take more than 15 minutes? The stationary had already been ready to collect the day before, but the van was in for MOT, as we know. So all he had got to do was load up and return. I looked in the back of the truck, and it appears that it wasn't unloaded when he returned yesterday, probably due to the murder. There are only a dozen boxes in there, each the size of a carton of photocopy paper, so t would not have taken long to load at the printers.

Let's be generous and allow 30 minutes to load, including a chat or cup of tea, plus another 15 minutes to get back here. That is a total of one hour for the round trip by my reckoning and 6.6 miles. Yet he didn't return until about 4:30 pm, and the mileage now is 56,359 miles, about 6 miles extra. So where else did he go in that extra

3 hours and 6 miles motoring? I think I'd better check it manually in my car tomorrow, rather than rely upon the phone app, but it seems suspicious."

"Capital!" exclaimed Webb. "And that boys and girls is what proper detective work often is – checking facts and not accepting what we are told. Well done! Before we dance in the streets, though, it's time to search the factory if you have finished your lunches. Be careful in there because there is lots of heavy machinery." They all moved off downstairs. Webb patted Newton on the back as they went. "Excellent work, but check it out thoroughly before we confront him. He could try and say he went to fill up with fuel. It may explain extra mileage, but never 3 hours in time."

The search in the factory section revealed an open carton of 100mm belts, all uncut with their paper sleeves. It appeared that one had been removed. They opened hatches on machines, looked underneath their stands and in the scrap metal cages to no avail. Peggy Catchpole searched the toilets and kitchen area attached to it without a result. Several packs of protective gloves were open around the factory floor and plenty of used ones in the rubbish bins. Finally, Webb decided that they had been thorough in their search and telephoned Eric Button to come and set the alarm and lock up. "You can have your building back now, thank you", he assured.

Conveyor Belt Corpse

Eric soon arrived, and the team departed back to H.Q. "There will be plenty more to do tomorrow", promised Webb ", but maybe you'd like to check out your theory first, DS Newton, before coming in?"

Chapter 6.

Whilst the police were searching Button Engineering, its staff were more in a limbo state. Eric Button sat at home, unable to settle to reading the newspaper or watching T.V. His wife had divorced him some years ago, having given up trying to change him. They had no children, so the company employees were interchangeable as his family. He knew that he was unlikely to get a call from DCI Webb to close up the building until late in the day because it was a large building to search. He worried what would become of him and the company: He was 54, two years younger than his brother but too old for many other companies to want to employ him. He would run the company for the moment, but it was unlikely to survive unless sales took a miraculous upswing or they produced a completely new product in two months. In any case, he had no enthusiasm for dealing with people. It had always been Sid who could talk with others. Even when he was younger, Sid was always more popular and better at sports, he thought sourly. Worst of all, he had married Kathleen, who Eric had loved but had not got the confidence to approach. What a sad legacy to his Father Edward's hard work, he thought. There wasn't even a competitor wanting to merge or take them over.

Gerry was equally gloomy but for different reasons: he knew that the row with his Father and lack of alibi made him a prime suspect for the murder, and he stayed in bed, drinking himself to oblivion. Even with the old man dead, he would have poor prospects at the company now. Moreover, once groomed to take over from him, he wasn't sure that he would now succeed, especially as Uncle Eric knew what happened in America. He had no close friends to talk to and felt alone and unloved.

Clive had slightly brighter thoughts. As his wife told him, with Gerry disgraced and Eric unlikely to want to become M.D., he had good prospects of being chosen for the job. He tried to say that the company wasn't doing very well, but as usual, she held sway. "Don't be so wet, Clive. For once in your life, grab an opportunity and be less of a mouse! Even if it is for a relatively short time, you would have control of the finances, and your Mother is likely to give you some of the shares that she inherits from your Father."

Gloria sat on the sofa at home opposite her Mother, both clutching mugs of coffee that were going cold and the wastepaper basket filling up with their tear-soaked tissues. "I can't believe it", repeated Kathleen again. "Who could have been so wicked to have done it?"

"For the last time, I don't know!" said Gloria irritably. "That is why we have the police. It is their job to find out." She wanted to support her Mother but felt inadequate. She was relieved that she had not been asked to tell Mother about the death yesterday but had spent most of the night listening to her, making hot drinks and avoiding thinking about her own situation. Looking out the window to the garden beyond, she could see Gordon trimming some bushes. He had arrived earlier that morning with the Bentley and offered his services which was kind, but there wasn't really anything she could ask him to do. She decided to go upstairs and take a long soak in the bath. It would at least give her a break from her Mother's histrionics.

Tim McCauley was not a member of the Button family, but having worked for them all his life, he felt a strong connection and loyalty. He was in his small terraced house on Walton High Street, just outside Felixstowe, where he lived as a bachelor alone. Unlike Eric's solitary home, he kept his neat and clean and enjoyed the rare luxury of a late breakfast. He fretted about his team of engineers and felt sure that none of them could be the culprit. He knew, though, that uncertainty, suspicions and change were never good for the team. Events like the murder could increase the possibility of accidents or inaccuracy as minds were distracted. When they returned, he must impress upon them the need to work well, which was what Sidney would have wanted.

Chapter 7. Saturday, June 11th, 2016

Peggy Catchpole had got into Police H.Q. extra early to submit her find of 'white powder' to the lab for analysis. When she got back into the office, she found Chris Winter already adding details to the whiteboard. Then the rest of the team arrived in quick succession, all eager to work on the case except for Colin Newton, who was already driving his V.W. Polo from Button Engineering to Warnocks Printers. He was timing it with an app on his mobile phone, having zeroed the tachograph before starting. He arrived outside the printers and stopped to check his readings. It had taken him 9 minutes, having kept to speed limits, pausing at junctions and being stopped by a traffic light along the way. The mileage to Trimley St. Martin was 2.8 miles, as he had expected. So where did the other 6 miles on the van's journey on Thursday come from? He pulled out a large scale map: if it was a return journey, the destination had to be about 3 miles away. He knew that Barker lived somewhere around Kirton, not far from Sidney's home. Had he simply popped home to put his feet up for a while? He was unlikely to be seen by his colleagues, who were all back at the factory.

Taking the obvious action, he checked Barker's address from the interview he had given and put the postcode into his sat-nav. Then, zeroing the tachograph again, he set off for Kirton. The destination turned out to be a slightly shabby looking mid-terrace house, 3.2 miles away. It took him 13 minutes, and he carried on past the home, not wanting Barker to see him snooping if he was at home.

So if the round trip mileage was 0.4 miles too far, maybe the destination could have been Sidney's home? He rang the office to find out where it was. Will Catesby answered and gave him the details, which he scribbled down. Thanking him, he told Will that he should be back at H.Q. in the next hour. Putting the tacho back to zero, he retraced his route back up the road that he had arrived on. Sidney Button's home was 0.2 miles away, set back from the road behind high hedges. "Yes!" he said aloud to himself in the car. The mileage was too much of a coincidence not to be the correct destination. With that, he returned triumphantly back to H.Q. at Martlesham, happily singing along with the radio.

At H.Q., Ron was knocking on the door of the lab. Dr Deborah Wilson looked up and saw him through the window. She smiled and beckoned him in. "Good morning DCI Webb," Deborah said brightly. "I know you policemen, you are only after one thing from a lady!" she laughed, reaching for a folder on the table.

"Ah, it is true, I'm afraid", admitted Ron, who was slightly embarrassed by her jokey manner. He always regarded the morgue and lab as very sombre places, but he supposed that staff would go mad if they stayed permanently serious in such places. It was probably not much different to some of the black humour shared between police officers after harrowing incidents.

Opening the folder, Deborah glanced inside to refresh her memory of the contents. She had dealt with two other autopsies since this one. "Mr Button had a slight heart defect, but a pacemaker had been fitted, which should have kept it stable. It did not have any role in the death as far as I could ascertain. It was strangulation, as we suspected. The hyoid bone, which is a u-shaped bone in the neck, was fractured, which rarely happens for any other reason. In addition, petechiae were present in the eyes. Sorry, that is red spots in layman's terms."

Ron produced the small sample of belt Eric Button had given him from his pocket. "Thank you. Could it have been done with a belt of this type, but up to two metres long?" he asked. She placed the toothed side against a close-up photograph of the neck of Sidney from the folder.

"That very certainly fits the bill: it is a perfect match to the contusions. I wish more of your colleagues could supply me with weapons at this stage," she added.

"On no, that is just a sample of a type used at Button Engineering. We still haven't found the actual belt used yet, despite it being reasonably tricky to conceal," admitted Ron.

"Given that the victim appeared to be sitting down, it wouldn't have taken a particularly tall or strong individual to kill him quite quickly", Dr Wilson continued. "It could have been a man or woman, and they were probably right-handed if you look at the more pronounced contusions on the left-hand side of the neck," she explained, indicating a point on another photo with her pen.

"That is very helpful. Thank you very much indeed, Doctor. Is it possible to narrow down the timeline at all?" asked Ron.

"He appeared to have eaten a ham sandwich not long before death, so that would probably put it after 1 pm if he ate his lunch then. However, the death was called in just after 3, so that gives you a 3-hour window."

"Yes, I found an empty lunch box in his desk drawer, so that would make sense," confirmed Ron. But, of course, he couldn't have eaten it much before then because he was occupied from 11 until about 12:40, as far as we can tell." Thanking the ever-pleasant Doctor once again, Ron returned to the squad room with the report in his hand.

When Colin walked through the squad room door, everyone was working hard typing up their individual logs from yesterday onto computers.

When he noticed that everyone already had a drink, he made himself a cup of tea from his personal supply of herbal teabags. Colin secretly hated making tea for the whole office and thought it was something only junior staff should do. Webb spotted him as he returned and came to join him. "How did you get on?" he asked.

"Brilliant!" exclaimed Colin.

"Oh well, you can fill us all in together in a moment. Now that you are back, we'll all get together and find out where we have all got and what needs doing next," responded Webb. The rest of the team had heard, and finishing sentences and saving work, they all angled their chairs towards Webb and the whiteboard.

"Let's start with the victim: Sidney Button, aged 56, MD of Button Engineering. Husband of Kathleen and father of three adult children who all worked for the company. He was last seen alive by the workers on the factory floor just after 12:30 and found at 3 o'clock dead, most likely strangled with a short, narrow conveyor belt. Pathology cannot establish a much shorter window of opportunity for the murder to have occurred. I have just got the report: it confirms that he was most likely to have been attacked from behind whilst sitting at his desk. So what does that tell us?"

"That he knew his attacker well enough to trust them walking behind him?" offered Peggy.

"Yes, very good. Now the bruising appears most evident on the left side of the neck, which suggests that was where the most substantial force was pulling. That would indicate a right-handed attacker if the belt was crossed behind the neck. Also, the hyoid bone in the neck was damaged, and there were red spots in the eyeballs, both consistent with strangling."

"Would that take a lot of force, sir? Could a woman have done it?" asked Chris Winter tentatively, breaking away from marking up the board.

"Good question," praised Webb. "I know from past cases it only takes about 4 pounds pressure on the jugular for death to happen within a minute. So yes, most women can manage that, particularly when the victim is sitting down: Even if they are short, they will still be in an excellent position to exert pressure from a standing position. Incidentally, the report also mentioned that Sidney had a heart pacemaker, but that wasn't the cause of death – it was definitely the strangulation.

Now let's consider the potential suspects: given that he probably knew his attacker, it is likely that it is someone from the company. We cannot totally exclude an outsider, as anyone could have entered by the door downstairs, gone up to the office and exited without being seen all in 10 minutes, and take the murder weapon with them.

However, an outsider is less likely to have a conveyor belt to hand without going into one of the downstairs rooms and potentially being seen. If murder were their intent, they would be more likely to carry their weapon with them from outside of the factory. As you have been working on Gordon Barker DS Newton, do you want to start with him?"

Newton nodded and stepped up to the board and jotted down sums copied from his notebook. "I explained to you I was suspicious about the amount of time that Barker took to pick up a few boxes of paper from a short distance away. So, checking out the mileage the van had travelled since the MOT, I travelled his likely route this morning. It is six miles more than it should be and three hours longer. Since he lives in Kirton, I drove on to his home: maybe he had gone home for a bit. It was slightly too far, but the distance exactly corresponded to Sidney and Kathleen Button's home, which is a striking coincidence. He works there and at the factory, but why wouldn't he mention going there as part of his alibi? If he hasn't lied to us, he certainly hasn't told us the whole truth."

Other members of the team nodded or checked his arithmetic in their heads. Then, finally, Will Catesby asked, "Do we know if Mrs Button was there?"

"That's a good point, DC Catesby", interrupted Webb. "I intended to go to see her later today. We shall ask her then, which may confirm whether Barker was there or not. If he was, it still doesn't put him in the clear – he could have killed Sidney before leaving the factory and deliberately stayed away until the murder was discovered. That leads us to motive. Why would he want to kill somebody who seemed to have been a reasonable employer? I got hold of the personal copies of personnel records kept by Sidney. There were some pencilled remarks beside them. Sidney had written 'makes himself useful' against Barker's notes."

"Any chance it could be Mrs Button?" asked Colin. "She could be the reason why he was coy about visiting the home in the afternoon while Sidney was at work. I wonder what time he actually visited the printers?" he mused. "I will check up on that later, sir", he added. "If she has her own car, she could have gone to the factory and done the deed before returning home. Mind you, if Barker was there, he may well have seen her comings and goings, which would be awkward for her. He could even be covering for her by not admitting he was there."

"I'm guessing that she has enough money to buy his silence if that was the case," suggested Webb. "Thank you, and good work. It is these sort of details that sometimes cause alibi's to unravel," responded Webb. "But let's not give up on the others quite yet", he added. "You know Clive Button and Tim McCauley were happy to say that Barker was away fetching stationary, but surely they would know it didn't take four hours?"

"Would they have any reason to shield him?" asked Peggy.

"Only if he knew something that they didn't want to come out", theorised Webb. "With Sidney out of the way, who stands to gain? I suppose Clive may manage to take over the company with father dead and brother disgraced. It could be a case of raw ambition, but why would McCauley back him up? They are each other's alibis for not going to murder Sidney. What if they did it jointly?" They claimed to be in a meeting together all afternoon in the accounts office."

"It would have to have been sometime earlier when Sheila wasn't at her desk to see them", commented Newton. "She did say that she leaves her desk to make tea, photocopy, do the post and so on when I interviewed her."

"Yes, but she is married to Clive," retorted Webb. "So she could be covering for him. It would be financially beneficial to her if he got promoted to Managing Director," he countered. "She could even have done it herself," he added. With all the doors closed, nobody is likely to see her come and go."

"What about Eric Button, sir?" asked Peggy. "I understand that he is the other director, with shares in the company. What if Eric has got fed up with his big brother lording it over him and appointing his children to fill all the important posts?"

"Good thinking, Catchpole", beamed Webb. He was pleased how all of the squad were doing some thinking and wanted to encourage it. "We only have his word that he was stuck in his room all afternoon. He could have easily have sneaked upstairs and into Sidney's office and back to his room without being seen. Yet another potential suspect!"

"There is a possible different possible motive for Eric Button, sir," suggested Newton. I found his old Xmas present list, and he bought Kathleen a far larger present than he did for his other relatives. Might he be attracted to her and want Sidney out of the way for that reason?"

"That is perfectly feasible", judged Webb. "It could even be a combination of the two factors. That leaves Gloria. What happened over your find, DC Catchpole?"

Pleased to get to her moment to shine finally, Peggy announced, "It was cocaine. There are fingerprints on the bag, which we can check out against Gloria's: they do not come up on the database. So if they are her's, she cannot allege that she doesn't know how it got into her locked draw. She also could have sneaked downstairs unseen. Do we bring her in?"

"Certainly not!" scoffed Webb in mock seriousness. It was your diligent find, so you have the responsibility of arresting her and getting the collar. If she were at work today, she would have discovered the drugs have disappeared and worry about it. But being at home instead, she will agitate all the more. So delay arresting her until I can sit in on the interview. She is more likely to tell us more when she has stewed a bit. Maybe in the meantime, you could apply for a warrant to search her home and see if there is any more. The fact that we can also look out for anything to link her or her Mother to the murder at the same time will be fortuitous. Thinking about it, if you can get the warrant in time, you could accompany DS Newton and me when we call later."

"She seemed quite a Daddy's girl when I interviewed her, but it could have been an act. I held the door for her to leave the office, so she wouldn't have had a chance to take the drugs with her. Or a murder weapon and rubber gloves come to that," informed Colin Newton.

"Except for his Masonic mates who we will leave to His Lordship later if all else fails, it seems that all the key employees are still in the frame for this," said Webb summing up the situation. "However, I think the factory staff alibi's back each other up, having read the statements taken by uniform now, so we will not pursue them at present. So some tasks for you to get on with:

DC Winter, check and see if there is any CCTV on the route to Bawdsey Ferry that may show Gerry or his car, and check around by his home as well. See if there is any social media stuff of interest on any of the suspects as well.

DC Catesby, apply for the phone logs and bank statements for Barker and Gerry. You may have to wait until Monday until they respond, but get the ball rolling at least.

DC Catchpole, you already have your orders.

DS Newton, you go and check out what time Barker visited the printer if they are open, then meet me outside the family home in Kirton at 5 pm. That should give DC Catchpole a chance to get a warrant, and she can meet us there. There is no work today at Button Engineering, being a Saturday, so I hope that Miss Goody Two Shoes Gloria will be home to explain herself and Mother to tell us about Barker.

There was a notepad on Sidney's desk with the initials 'G.B.?' It probably refers to Gerry Button, who he was troubled with, but it occurred to me that it could also refer to Gloria Button or even Gordon Barker. We are waiting for the lab to come back with anything else they can tell us about the pad and the laptop. Can you chase them up, DS Newton, please?

It also still bothers me that we haven't got the murder weapon."

"About that, sir." It was Peggy Catchpole speaking up.

"Yes, what are you thinking?" asked Ron.

"Well, I thought I'd see what I could find out about the belts on the internet. They generally have two markings on the reverse side. One is CE, and it is supposed to signify that the belt is made to EU standards for health, safety, and environmental protection. Apparently, though, the Chinese started making some inferior belts with CE on them. When asked about them, they said it stood for China Export, which is a bit cheeky. The problem is that CE only applies to machines, not consumables like tyres or belts, so there isn't the same protection, and they sometimes make them under the same or similar company names. However, most reputable companies also print serial numbers that can be traced down to a manufacturer, factory, and shift for quality assurance purposes.

I saw the ones in the factory, and they were like that in the open box. They were bound with a paper sleeve that said 'Nastva Ltd' and had a CE mark plus a serial number. The top one was numbered 14324679, and half the box was already gone. Beneath it, the other belts were numbered in ascending order, 14324680 and so on. I know you said that there were more in the stationery cupboard. So if we had the serial number of the top one from there, we could predict the serial number of the last one taken. So if the murder weapon was found, it should be possible to work out which of the two sources it came from, upstairs or downstairs, so long as it wasn't an odd older one that had been left lying around. What do you think, sir?" Peggy waited expectedly for a response. After a pause, a rare smile forced its way across Rons slightly dour face.

"I think that is an admirable bit of thinking and research you have done there, which is an example to us all. I must admit that I didn't think of that. However, I brought back the top belt and wrapper from the stationery cupboard as a reference sample! Wait here, and I'll get it from my office." So saying Ron went to his office to retrieve it. Colin gave Peggy a big wink and said, "Excellent!" The combined praise meant a great deal to her, and she looked forward to telling her policeman husband when she got home.

Ron Webb reappeared, holding the belt and wrapper. "14324205", he exclaimed. So the belt above it should be 14324204 then. Note them down on the board plus the ones from the shop floor. Any other suggestions like that last one? Or questions even?" When nobody responded, he said, "Let's get on with it then!" Just then, a phone rang. DC Catesby picked it up.

"Serious Crime Unit, DC Catesby. May I help you?" There was a pause then. "Yes, sir. Right away, sir – I will tell him." Before he could pass the message on, Ron looked upwards, rolled his eyes and said, "Don't tell me, His Lordship wants to see me." DC Catesby nodded. "Oh well, thanks to all your hard work, at least I have some positive things to tell him."

A few minutes later, he had climbed the stairs and knocked on the door of his boss, the man officially known as Detective Superintendent Hardy.

"Well, DCI Webb, how is this Sidney Button case progressing?" he asked.

"We are making some progress, sir. From our initial enquiries, I believe that the murderer is someone working at the company. We are also reasonably certain that the murder weapon was a narrow section of conveyor belt, but it has not yet been found despite an intensive search. The main problem is that all of the main employees of the company have a possible motive to want Sidney Button gone, and most have good alibis. However, my team have come up with a couple of good leads, which we are now following up."

"Glad to hear it, Webb", pronounced Hardy. "The press is inevitably interested, especially as he was a respected member of the local community." (And a Mason thought Ron privately.) But, then this massive operation at Weybread costs a fortune and DCI Gray has little to show so far for it so far. I appreciate you using your team in place of SOCO in the search. Do you think that they were able to do such as effective job" Hardy quizzed?

"Yes, sir, they took extra care, and I gave them plenty of time as they are not so experienced. However, the team are very well motivated, all of them. Several have shown good initiative in this case, but I was especially pleased with the way that DC Catchpole has been using her head and going 'above and beyond.'

"Excellent, I am sure you set them a good example. That Catchpole is up for her Sergeant's exams soon, isn't she?"

"Yes and keen as mustard – I bet she will go far", answered Ron. There was rarely harm in getting his officers from getting recognition for good work.

"Very good, carry on and get me a result as soon as you can. I'm relying upon you, DCI Webb!"

'Patronising git!' whispered Ron to himself as he slowly walked back down the stairs.

Chapter 8.

The printers had been closed when Newton called, which wasn't too surprising for a Saturday. It meant that he was early in parking up near to the Button's home in Kirton. Unfortunately, Catchpole was frustrated by JPs being off sailing, playing golf or on holiday, so she failed to get a search warrant in time to take to Kirton with Webb. "Don't worry about it – you were only in with a slim chance anyway. We may not need it if Gloria comes clean. Accompany me to Kirton regardless," invited Webb.

It was good to have a passenger who didn't chatter ceaselessly like Newton and wasn't afraid of sharing his humbugs. "Didn't your Mum ever tell you not to take sweeties from strangers in cars" he joked. "They don't come much stranger than me!" He knew that Catchpole was disappointed at not getting the warrant in time and wanted to put her more at ease. She chuckled at his joke.

"If we do get the chance to search Gloria's room, I would like you to do it, please", he continued. "It would be less intrusive than a male going through her underwear and so on. Then charge her and make the arrest if she is there."

"Yes, of course," acknowledged Catchpole. She had initially thought her boss to be a grizzled old-timer, but every now and again, he surprised her with a more sensitive side.

"You have been working well," said Webb. "I told His Lordship today, so you keep at it with those Sergeant exams. If you want to know anything, ask DS Newton or me.

"Thank you, sir, I really appreciate that," said Peggy.

During the journey, Webb reflected to himself what other information they had gleaned today: SOCO had examined Sidney's laptop. It had an electronic diary on it, showing his last appointment with Gerry, but nothing more. Previous entries and emails did not reveal any potential enemies or concerns. The notepad drew a blank also. Being a Saturday, Catesby had not been able to get any information from banks or phone companies and would have to wait until Monday.

However, DC Winter had managed to check out some social media accounts: Gloria seemed to be on everything, including Facebook, Twitter and Instagram but did not seem to post much herself. There were a few photos of her with her girlfriends and some holiday snaps, but little of interest. Gerry had a Facebook account but mainly used it to discuss football and arrange meet-ups with friends for drinks or restaurants. The rest of the family appeared shy of social media. There was no trace of anything for Tim McCauley, but Gordon Barker used Facebook to swap news with numerous family members in Australia but almost nothing else.

They pulled up in front of Newton's car. "The printers were closed for the day," he told them. "I will get back onto them next Monday morning."

"Right, I will take the lead with Mrs Button. DC Catchpole has been told to deal with Gloria, and you DS Newton join in when you want," instructed Webb.

"I doubt if she is there," informed Newton. Her car is gone."

"Rats!" exclaimed Catchpole as they walked between two high hedges and down a long driveway. Next, she rang the doorbell of the large, detached five bedroom period home. Eventually, the door was opened by Kathleen Button, wearing a black dress and subtle make-up and perfume. Warrant cards were produced, introductions made, and she invited them into a comfortable, elegant lounge.

"My condolences for your loss, Mrs Button," said Webb, and the others nodded in agreement.

"Thank you, it is appreciated," she replied in a refined and elegant voice. "Of course, it was so unexpected. Dear Eric told me the ghastly details. Have you arrested anyone yet?"

"Not yet, but we are following up some leads at present," replied Webb in a practised phrase that had served him well over the years. It told the enquirer that an investigation was underway without giving away any details. "Are you being supported by your daughter Gloria?" he asked. "Am I right in believing that she lives here with you?"

"Yes, she does, but she is off with some friends for the weekend somewhere in the country. They had been planning it for weeks, so I do not expect her to be home until late on Sunday. I insisted that she still went to it. She is the only one not to have flown the nest of my three children, and sometimes I despair she ever will! Still, she is a comfort when she is here," Kathleen concluded. Peggy tried to hide her disappointment. It didn't seem appropriate to ask to search her room if she wasn't under arrest or here to give permission.

"Do you know if your husband had any enemies or recent disputes with anyone?" Ron continued.

"No, I shouldn't think so, although I forbade him to discuss boring business in the home, so I don't know much about who he dealt with there. He often went off to the Masons and occasionally dragged me with him when they permitted women to a social event. Boring lot! But then he fitted in so well," she added cattily. "You can probably gather that I am not heartbroken. He was so pompous! It was a wonder I haven't strangled him myself on occasions, although I hasten to add I didn't do it. I was stuck here at home as usual when it happened."

"Was anyone else here at the time, Mrs Button?" chipped in Newton.

She paused and was visibly considering her answer by the looks that crossed her face. Then turning to Newton, she said, "You naughty man! You are trying to get me to come up with what I think they call 'an alibi.' We are quite isolated from the village here, so who would see me? I cannot drive, so I would not get far."

Trying to be a little subtle, Webb asked, "Couldn't you get the chauffeur Gordon Barker to drive you when your husband was at work?"

"Well, yes, I could, but it would be an awful waste of his time, don't you think?"

"I understood that your husband pays part of his wages himself for chauffeuring and household jobs," said Newton, eyeing Webb for approval to continue. Webb gave the briefest of winks.

"Since he got arrested for drunk driving after a Masonic do in London, he was banned, so he had to have Gordon to drive him. I think it made him feel grand, sitting in the back of the Bentley. As it happened in London, it wasn't reported around here, so he blamed it on his heart for the benefit of the public, too proud to admit he could do anything wrong. Huh! That's a laugh – he hadn't got a heart!" Kathleen exclaimed. "I shall sell that gas guzzler as soon as I can, learn to drive and get myself something sporty. At last, I am free to be my own woman."

"Free to find a more suitable partner, maybe?" suggested Peggy brightly.

"Yes, that as well," said Kathleen defiantly. "You might think me wicked for thinking such things so soon after Sidney's death, but in a way, he has been dead to me for years. I would have been better going with dear old Eric all those years ago."

"His brother?" prompted Peggy.

"Oh yes, he was keen on me, but Sidney at the time was more sporty and dashing and stole me away from him. I was a foolish young girl, easily flattered and lived to regret it. Eric has always held a torch for me but was too polite and gentlemanly to cuckold his brother. Regrettably, he has left it too late now."

"So excuse me being curious, but has he already got a rival again? I notice that you are wearing make-up and a beautiful dress. Did you intend to see somebody this evening?" asked Peggy tentatively, hoping she wasn't overstepping the mark.

"You are too clever to be under these men!" announced Kathleen with a derisive laugh. "Yes, I am. It is the same man who was with me in bed last Thursday afternoon. I'm guessing that you are investigating where Gordon was when the murder happened. Well, I cannot let him get into trouble on account of me, so I had better admit that yes, he was here. As I said, I wouldn't want him to waste his time driving me around! He is far more useful in the bedroom!" She gave a wink.

"We are not here to judge your personal life," assured Peggy. "But it would help if you could tell us when he arrived.

"It must have been about 1 o'clock I should think because I had just switched off the television. The news was about to come on, and it is all about the EU and football hooligans in Russia, and I am not interested. Gordon left in a hurry before 4. He had got to collect something from Trimley on the way back to the factory, then drive Sidney home, and had not realised how late it was."

"That is very helpful, thank you. It maybe doesn't tell us who killed Sidney, but it sort of lets me know who didn't," said Webb, standing and preparing to leave. The rest took his cue, and they said their goodbyes. Kathleen watched them walk back down the drive from the front door, presumably awaiting another visit from Gordon. As they got back to the cars, Peggy apologised. "Sorry if I jumped in with both feet there, but no woman, however posh, spends the evening alone in a nice dress, stockings and make-up to watch the telly alone."

"Very true, I'm sure," replied Webb. "Using your superior knowledge about the fairer sex was useful, and you posed questions it would have been much harder for a man to ask without causing insult."

"I agree", chipped in Newton. "I would probably get my face slapped! I will still double-check with the printer on Monday, though."

"It looks like I will have to catch Gloria at work, sir, doesn't it?" asked Peggy.

"Yes, leave it until Monday. She will not know the drugs have been found until then anyway, and you can apply for a warrant after you have arrested her," confirmed Webb. "Yes, Newton, do check the printers; let's keep it tight. Gordon could still have killed Sidney Button before seeing Kathleen, so timing is still essential.

Right, let's get home. My wife promised steak and kidney pudding tonight, and it is 6 o'clock already! See you sometime on Monday, Newton. I will drop you back at Martlesham Catchpole." Then he stopped getting into the car. "Newton, sorry, but could you drop off Catchpole instead? I have just thought; If Kathleen is expecting Gordon tonight, she will ensure that his story agrees with hers. So I will nip up to his home first to intercept him and get his version of the timetable. I still cannot believe that those other managers didn't notice how long he took."

"Are you sure you don't want me to do it?" asked Newton. "Your steak and kidney pud is waiting, and I have only got a frozen pizza when I get home."

"No, that will keep, but thanks for offering. It shouldn't take me long. It will be one more little piece of the jigsaw. The trouble with the jigsaw in these investigations is that there is an infinite number of pieces, no corners or straight edges to make it easier, and part of the sky is missing!"

"Very profound, sir!" commented Newton and gave him directions to Gordon's home and left with Peggy. He had almost bored her silly with details of his exercise routine on the way back before he dropped her off to pick up her car back at base. She was not impressed.

DCI Webb quickly found Gordon Barker's home and was glad to see that the lights were still on at the mid-terraced house. But, knocking on the door, he had to wait a while before Gordon appeared. "Sorry, but I was upstairs getting ready to go out. I gave a statement to your man the other day – what do you want now? I'm running late."

"Oh, I'm sure Kathleen will wait a little while for you. Now, if you'd like to let me in, I will be as quick as you can, and yes, I know that you were with Kathleen last Thursday afternoon." Gordon turned without saying a word, and Ron followed him inside to a shabby living room with a worn pair of armchairs, old TV and a trolley acting as a table. Gordon sat down, and Ron followed.

"You seem to know a lot of what I have been doing! So what's this all about?" said Gordon sharply but looking confused.

"I am not much interested in your love life Mr Barker," said Ron calmly. "I am, however, interested to know where everybody really was last Thursday afternoon. What time did you leave the factory?"

"I don't know exactly, but I had my sandwiches with the lads in the factory. Their break is 12-12:30 pm, so it must have been a few minutes after that. I drove the van straight to the Button's home and parked it around the side."

"OK, so when did you leave there?" asked Ron.

"That I do know. I hadn't noticed it was late because I had taken my watch off. By the time I realised it was a quarter to four. So I raced off and got to the printers at just after four. The gaffer there was annoyed because he wanted to leave sharpish to go out somewhere and had expected me earlier. So I loaded up as fast as I could and got back to the factory at about four-thirty. That was when I found out that Sidney was dead."

"How come the Clive Button and Tim McCauley didn't query why you took so long then?" followed on Ron.

"They daren't! Clive's office door is solid, so you can't see in it, and everyone knocks before entering. One day though, I had to pull up the van on the opposite side of the road outside because a lorry had stopped across the entrance. While I was waiting for it to move, I could clearly see Clive cuddling with Tim through the upstairs window of the accounts office. I dropped a couple of choice remarks later, and that keeps them off my back in case I tell anyone. So nothing illegal in that is there?" Gordon queried aggressively.

"No, I don't expect so, but anything more might be construed as blackmail", replied Webb with a sigh. "That will be all for now, Mr Barker, but we may need to speak again, so don't stray too far, will you?" he added with just the right tinge of menace. "I will leave you to your romantic evening."

Ron got back in the car and thought what a bit of low life he was, but nothing was worth pursuing with him at present. So he comforted himself with a humbug and headed home.

Chapter 9. Sunday 12th June 2016

None of the team had been requested to work on Sunday, so they all had a day off. It was a rare treat for Peggy to be off at the same time as her husband, so they laid in bed late and went out to a country pub for lunch. They ended up discussing work inevitably, but they managed to agree on a future holiday destination between them. They now had to try to book leave for the same weeks, not an easy task.

As usual, Colin Newton headed for the gym and had a stroll back along the waterside development where he had his flat in Ipswich. Masses of expensive yachts were moored at the marina, and a noisy crowd sat at tables on the quayside outside a bar and restaurant. The chink of halyards against masts was almost drowned out.

There were plenty of couples out, and it made Colin think about his situation again. He hadn't been very successful in asking out women on dates: some didn't like the idea of a boyfriend on shifts or in the police, and he had been given the brush off once too often. Thinking positively, Colin thought again about registering for one of those dating apps that seemed so popular. At least people were looking for a partner there, so he resolved to do it that very afternoon. When he got back to his flat, he went through the process and soon looked through the local contacts pictures and blurb. He was surprised to find that Gloria Button was on there. *'Single attractive Marketing Manager, 26 seeks exciting partner. No stuffed shirts need to apply!'*

Why shouldn't she be on there? Young free and single, but it worried him that he might have hooked up with someone using cocaine without knowing it if he had not recognised her. That would not do his police career much good, let alone his love life. So he shut down the app and tried to watch TV instead. It mainly was murder mysteries, and so he flicked through the channels trying to find something else. The 'whodunnits' irritated him with their inaccurate police procedures and easy coincidences. Eventually, he found a documentary about crocodiles and settled down to watch that.

Chris Winter wasn't even trying to date at present. Having split up from girlfriend Sara a few months ago, he was taking a break and was around his mate Simon's flat playing a computer game with a high incidence of explosions, gunfire, aliens and mayhem. They had a couple of beers from the fridge, and a takeaway was being delivered later. Just the sort of day to forget about work, women, money or anything else stressful.

On the other hand, Will Catesby was birdwatching in a local woodland, which was his way of relaxing. He felt the warm sunshine on his back as he peered through his binoculars. There were no particular rare birds about, but he was pleased to watch a treecreeper work its way almost vertically down a tree trunk while probing the bark for insects. Later on, he would return home for a stew he had put on in the slow cooker and settle down to a film on tv that he wanted to watch.

Ron Webb was a traditionalist and looked forward to a Sunday roast cooked by his wife Alice with all the trimmings whenever he managed to get a Sunday off. At present though, he was attending to the roses in his garden, which were a particular passion of his. There were some very showy specimens that he fertilised, pruned and cosseted, but this was the time of year when some of the older varieties were blooming. They had much more of a scent than the newer hybrid varieties, and Ron went to the corner of the garden where they grew to enjoy their fragrance. He was sadly disappointed when instead, he smelt the sour odour of cat excrement. Disgusted, he went in for a cup of tea. "Damn cats", he complained to Alice. "They have spoilt the corner where the Peace roses grow," he complained.

"They frighten off the birds from my feeders and bird table as well," said Alice, appreciating his distress. She was about to carry on this rare conversation with her frequently absent husband when he suddenly charged from the kitchen saying 'that's it, that must be it!' to himself. "That job has finally sent you off your rocker then?" she inquired after his retreating back. "It has given me an idea for the case I am working on, dear," he said excitedly.

"Well, I'm glad you are happy again", replied Alice, "wash your hands from the garden. I am just about to dish up dinner." After dinner, he made a call to Peggy's home phone. It went to ansaphone. "I am really sorry to disturb your day off, but don't go to the factory tomorrow before speaking to me," he said.

Chapter 10. Monday, June 13th, 2016

As the police had surmised, the staff had returned to work at Button Engineering on Monday morning. Tim McCauley unlocked and switched off the burglar alarm just before the engineers arrived at 8 am. There was a lot of low talking, despondent looks, and nobody seemed keen to make a start. But, having known them for years, this was what Tim expected, so he called them together for a quick pep talk. "Look, lads", he began, "we are all obviously upset at the death of Sidney Button. The Police are continuing their investigations, so we hope they catch his killer soon. If any of you know anything, however trivial, that might have any bearing on their investigation, you can come and see me in private at any time. He wasn't a bad boss, and we must bear in mind that some of our colleagues around the company are his close relatives, so be a bit sensitive to that if they come in here. If I know old Sidney Button, he was proud of this company and his workforce, so let's do him proud and get back to work. It is what he would have wanted!" The men nodded and switched on machines and got out their toolboxes. Michael Dooley walked over to Tim as he headed back to his office. "Can I check something about my apprenticeship with you, please, Tim?" he asked, loud enough to be overheard.

"Of course you can, Michael," replied Tim. "Come over to the office now before I get distracted by all I've got to catch up on."

Once inside the office, Tim invited Michael to sit down on the only other chair. "Now, what is it?" he asked.

"Well, I don't want to appear silly, and it may be something completely nonsense, so I don't want to waste anyone's time," said Michael falteringly.

"You let me be the judge of that, Michael," reassured Tim. "You're a good man, and I hope that I always make time to listen."

"Well," explained Michael, sounding a little more confident, "about a week ago, I emptied all the bins in the factory section into a drum and carried it to the backdoor. It was mid-morning, and I was going to empty it into the dumpster in the carpark as usual, in advance of the refuse collection the next day, so it must have been a Tuesday because they come on Wednesdays. I was just turning the key in the door when I heard raised voices outside. Not wanting to get involved, I kept behind the door, but I could see that it was Gerry Button and Gordon Barker. Gerry looked furious and had grabbed Gordon by the neck of his shirt. Then Gordon shoved him away and was pointing at him in what looked like a threat. I couldn't hear what was being said, but you could see that they were furious. Finally, Gerry walked over to his car and sped off, and

Gordon got into the van and drove off a minute or two later. I thought that if Gordon wanted to complain about Gerry, then he was quite able to do it for himself, and it was up to him.

Anyway, Gordon returned later and sat having his sandwiches with us all and didn't say anything, so I didn't comment. Getting this apprenticeship has been really important to me, and I don't want to get involved in other people's quarrels. It may have nothing to do with what happened on Thursday, but I thought that it best that I mentioned it now in case it was important." The young chap looked quite relieved to have got the matter off his chest.

"You did the right thing, Michael," assured Tim. "It's always best to keep out of other peoples arguments, but given the situation, it was wise to tell me now. I will discreetly pass on a message to the police, and they can ask questions if they think it is relevant to their enquiry. Otherwise, don't mention it to anyone else. You just get on and pass that final exam at college, eh? Any help you need just come and ask me. Your practical work is first class, so let's make sure you clear the final hurdle!" With that, he ushered Michael out of the door and sat thinking.

Tim wondered what it had been about? Gerry didn't usually have much to do with the engineers unless he wanted something. On the other hand, Gordon was involved with the factory engineers, office staff and worked for the Button family. So the row may be nothing to do with the company, but he decided to pass the information on to the police anyway. Tim had reason to dislike Gordon, so serve him right if he got grief for it. It took a while for him for his call to be directed to the correct Police department. After the tenth cycle of the Four Seasons tune and a message telling him that his call was important, he eventually spoke with DC Catesby, who promised to inform his boss straight away and ensure that the source was kept discreet if possible.

Around that same time, Gloria Button arrived at the office a quarter of an hour before her usual 9 am start. She closed her door and went straight to her locked draw with the key from the pencil pot before even taking her coat off. The plastic bag was missing from the back of the marker pen wallet, and she knew that it must have been found during the Police search the previous day. Her heart raced, and she sat down, trying to think what to do, but her mind went blank. It was half an hour before she took off her coat and hung it up. Then, opening the door and crossing to the kitchen area, she made herself a strong cup of black coffee with two spoons of sugar in to stifle the shock of being found out. Finally, she scuttled back to her office before Sheila could engage her in conversation: Gloria could not face anyone at present. When there was a knock on her door, she jumped, half expecting the police but it was Uncle Eric. "I just popped my head around to see how you were doing," he said kindly.

"Finding it hard to concentrate," she said truthfully. "Have the police been back in touch?"

"No, they rang me Friday to come and lock up the place in the late afternoon, but other than that, nothing", he answered. "Gerry has left an email which said that he didn't feel good enough to come in. Are you sure you are ok? Go home if you don't feel well – you look as if you are still in shock, Gloria. I dare say that your Mother could do with the company at the moment. I can manage things here for a few days."

"If you are sure? Thank you, I think I will. There is nothing urgent that needs doing on my desk," said Gloria, glad of some breathing space. Eric walked off to check on how Clive was holding up.

Clive greeted Eric as if it was any other morning. He was generally unexcitable and was checking figures on his computer screen, an activity with which he was comfortable. When Eric asked him if he was alright, he calmly stated that he was sure that they would all get on with their jobs as usual. After that, Eric left and checked in with Sheila. "Any work queries for Sidney, you can put through to me in my room," he instructed. "I will try to deal with anything that crops up until we can get sorted out," he assured. "Oh, by the way, Gerry is not in, and I have just sent Gloria home again."

"Thank you. Any news from the police?" she asked.

"No, nothing yet", Eric replied and made his way downstairs to the sanctity of his workroom where things were more familiar. Except, of course this morning they were not, with his logically dispersed filing system compacted into two mixed piles of paper by the police. He groaned.

Chapter 11.

Colin Newton was outside the printers when it opened at 9 am on Monday. The manager confirmed that the driver from Button Engineering had picked up some work after 4 pm last Thursday. "I remember it because I wanted to get away early to be there for my daughter's 5th birthday party. The company had said that they couldn't pick it up on Wednesday but would call on Thursday afternoon. I generally help people out with stuff to their vehicles, but I must admit I left him to do it himself while I was locking up."

"Thank you very much indeed, sir – that was very helpful," said Colin as he left. Before he could get back to his car, a call came in for him on his mobile phone. It was Webb. He asked how he had got on, and Colin told him. "Can you keep down in Felixstowe at present, please?" Ron asked. Meet DC Catchpole and me at the factory. I will explain why when we get there."

"Sure, boss," agreed Newton and drove at a leisurely pace to the burger van on the industrial estate, just up the road from Button Engineering. He bought a cup of coffee and sat drinking it in his car until the others arrived. When they did arrive, Webb explained the situation and handed him a large evidence bag and a walking stick. Then together, they drove the short distance into the carpark at the rear of Button's. Getting out of the cars, they went over to the dumpster bin. There wasn't a lot in it, and certainly no conveyor belt or gloves. It seems that Michael Dooley had not yet emptied the bins since the last refuse collection.

"Good, nothing has been dumped from the factory yet, so I reckon the murder weapon is still inside", commented Ron. He led them around to the unlocked front entrance of the building. Inside, Peggy trotted up the stairs and turned right through the door to the office suite. She was confronted by Sheila, who was sorting post at her desk. When she said who she wanted to see, Sheila apologised. "Sorry dear, she was in, but Mr Eric Button sent her home again because she wasn't coping very well. Is there anything I can help you with?"

"No, thank you", replied Peggy tersely and returned downstairs. She called to her colleagues, "she's gone home!"

"Never mind, catch her there later. Come here, and let's see if my theory is any good," instructed Webb. All three put on protective gloves, and Newton handed her the large evidence bag. He then hooked the cat litter tray from under the stairs with the walking stick. Then he pushed the straight end of the walking stick into the tray through the clean white granules. "Hopefully, it hasn't been used by Brunel yet," he murmured.

"I don't think he ever uses it," said Webb. "There is no smell from this area the other day, which you would expect. It is the same today, thankfully." Then, finally, Newton struck something solid and started pushing litter away to reveal it. "I knew it!" said Webb peering in with a satisfied grin. "The belt!"

Peggy held the bag open, flat to the floor, and Newton handed the stick back to Webb. He carefully picked up the litter tray and slid it into the bag, where Peggy sealed it tightly and brought out a pen to label it. Then Ron knocked on Eric's door. "Sorry to bother you, and it may sound a daft question, but did you say that Sheila Button put out the food and litter for Brunel?"

"Why, yes. We thought it was best if only one person was responsible so that he doesn't get missed out or fed twice. Unless Sheila is away, it is always her job. What on earth has this got to do with Sid's murder?"

"Quite a bit as it happens," said Ron. "Is Gerry Button in the office today?"

"No, he called in sick, so he should be at home," answered Eric.

Ron Webb started to ascend the stairs. Eric and the other officers followed him. As they entered the office suite, Sheila was still at her desk. "I told you that Mr Button sent Gloria home," she said to Peggy. "Isn't that right, Eric?" she asked as Peggy moved around the desk behind her.

"Sheila Button, I am arresting you under suspicion of murdering Sidney Button on Thursday 9th of June, 2016", announced DCI Webb. He officially cautioned her as DC Catchpole grabbed her wrists from behind and slipped them into waiting handcuffs. Uniform was summoned to take her away and soon arrived. By then, they had an audience of other staff, including her husband Clive, who was making a polite protest about the arrest of his wife. She didn't say a thing as she was led away.

Seeing Gordon Barker again, Webb walked over to him and took him to one side. "I believe that you had an altercation with Gerry Button in the carpark a week ago. Would you care to tell me what it was about?"

"Nothing much. He doesn't like me parking the van too close to his posh car, in case it gets scratched, the jumped-up little ponce!" was the swift reply.

"A bit violent, wasn't he?" suggested Webb.

"All bluster!" retorted Barker.

"So you will not be pressing charges then?" asked Webb. "No? We'll leave it at then for the moment, shall we?" Barker glared and walked off.

"Lying through his teeth", commented Newton.

"Almost certainly," responded Webb. "Sheila Button only had to wait until Wednesday night to empty the litter tray into the dumpster, and the refuse men would have taken away the murder weapon for her early the following day. I bet the belt came from the stationary cupboard.

Now, DS Newton, can you accompany DC Catchpole to apprehend the elusive Gloria Button, who we can only hope is now back home? I will go and see Gerry Button and ask him for his opinion of the scuffle with Barker. I will see you back at HQ later."

Just then, DS Chris Winter drove up and spent a few minutes talking to Webb. "Well done, Winter!" said Webb. "You'd better follow me to Gerry Button's place."

Chapter 12.

Gerry answered the door to DCI Webb and DC Winter in a less inebriated state than he had been on the previous visit but looked washed out. He was unshaven and didn't look as though he had much sleep. "What's up?" he inquired as he sat down opposite Webb.

"We have just arrested Sheila on suspicion of the murder."

"Christ!" exclaimed Gerry. "Who'd have thought it? I would never have suspected her. I mean, I must have been a more likely candidate, with no alibi," said a relieved Gerry.

"You can thank my officer here for providing you with one then," commented Webb.

"You didn't think anyone had noticed you when you went to the Bawdsey Ferry point last Thursday. That is still true, but someone did see your rather distinctive car in the Ferry Café carpark. Unfortunately, there is no CCTV in the area, but I talked to the café owner this morning. One of her staff is a bit of a petrol-head and remembered seeing your motor parked up all afternoon from about 12:15 when it arrived until he left to go home at 4:30."

"Yes, I did leave it there, but I didn't go into the café. It is the only place you can safely park around there. I went and sat on the beach, staring out at the sea and trying to work out what to do," recalled Gerry.

"So it seems," confirmed Webb."But it doesn't explain why you had a furious argument with Gordon Barker in the carpark behind the factory a week or so ago. What was that about?"

"You know about that?" quizzed Gerry. "I was telling him to leave my sister alone."

"Was he trying to 'become familiar' with her then?" asked Webb, raising an eyebrow. In the background, Winter smiled to himself at Webb's polite phrasing. He would have probably said, 'was he trying to shag her?

"No, nothing like that. Look, to tell the truth, Barker had got hold of drugs for me in the past. I was never a regular user, but one time I scared myself, and I have stuck to alcohol since then.

The other time I saw Barker go to Gloria's office late in the afternoon and go in. I knew that she was going to a party after work. I thought it unusual because he doesn't have much work involvement with her other than occasionally driving her and Dad to work. Anyway, he emerged a few minutes later, looking smug and putting something into his wallet. I saw Gloria before she left work, and her pupils were dilated, and she was chatting very excitably. I thought I could also see some grains of white powder on her jacket. It was evident that she had been snorting coke. It was no good tackling her about it then in that state, and she would have probably told me to go away. I think she was aware that I'd used drugs in the past. I even got expelled from school for smoking cannabis with another lad. I didn't want her to end up a regular drug user – she's my little sister, and I care about what happens to her. So I tried to warn off Barker in the carpark the next day, but he told me I shouldn't be such a hypocrite. He had supplied me at times in the past. Am I in trouble?"

"No, but I think he is," said Webb. "One of my officers is at your sister's home by now arresting her for drug possession. Some cocaine was found in her draw during the police search."

"Oh no! That was what I was trying to avoid. Mum will be devastated," said Gerry. "I'd better go over and see her later," he added.

After they had left Gerry, Webb got on the phone to Newton and told him what had transpired. He was already at the home in Kirton with Catchpole, who had arrested and cautioned Gloria. She had not denied that the cocaine was hers. When they said that the bag was being fingerprinted, she consented to them searching her bedroom. Nothing else was found. When asked who her dealer was, she had defiantly said, "Probably some nameless man down the pub – isn't that what they usually say to you?"

Conveyor Belt Corpse

Newton went back with the new information and said to her, "We know it was Barker who sold you the cocaine." She replied, "He seems to be Mr Fixit for everyone, including me. Yes, of course, it was him."

Back outside Gerry's block of flats, it was time for more action: "Right!" said Webb decisively to Winter. "Let's go back to the factory and arrest that nasty little toerag Barker for dealing Class A, shall we? Seeing as you worked hard to verify Gerry's alibi, you can have the credit of arresting him!"

"Thank you very much, sir," responded Winter, and they each drove back to the factory. Eric was just taking a mug of tea into his room as they arrived. "Sorry, Mr Button, but we are just about to arrest another one of your employees: Gordon Barker. Do you know where he is, please?"

"Yes, he was up a ladder replacing a strip light in the upstairs kitchen. Don't tell me he was involved with the murder as well?"

"No sir, suspected of dealing drugs, which is nearly as bad in my book," commented Webb as he followed Winter upstairs. "They kill a lot more than one person," he added. "I have to tell you that your niece Gloria has just been arrested for possession as well."

"Oh no!" murmured Eric, shaking his head slowly and sadly. "She is such a lovely young lady and the image of her Mother. I had better call the company solicitor for her."

DC Winter asked Gordon to step down from the ladder and arrested him for dealing Class A drugs. After a caution, he was taken away by uniformed officers. Later, Winter obtained a warrant for a search of Barker's home, where a quantity of drugs and a bundle of banknotes, scales and jiffy bags were found. His phone was examined and found to contain a dozen sets of initials in the contacts, with which he was suspected of trading drugs. However, he was too scared to reveal who his supplier was. As a result, he was facing a custodial prison sentence. "I cannot think of a more deserving case," commented Webb.

Gloria Button appeared in court soon after her arrest. She was fined and put on probation. Her Mother and Gerry escorted her away afterwards, and she returned home with them. "You stupid girl!" admonished her Mother. "It seems, though, as if we have all had secrets in this family, so it is about time I was honest with you both. She told them about Gordon Barker and how she felt that he had betrayed her trust in selling drugs to them both. Apparently, he had offered them to Gloria when he ferried her home after a party one night, when she was the worse for wear. "I should have stood up to your father too", she confided, "when he forced you, Gerry, into a job you hated and when he objected to any young man that you brought home, Gloria. He bullied all of us in his way."

Chapter 12. Tuesday 14ᵗʰ June 2016

No valuable further evidence had been obtained from the telephone log of Gerry, but Gordon Barkers revealed a string of texts to customers and one contact that looked to be his supplier. The Drugs Squad received the telephone numbers from Webb with thanks. Barker's bank account looked very healthy compared with his wages from Button Engineering, with frequent cash deposits. Gerry's bank account was an excellent example of someone living beyond their means, especially if one didn't earn much commission to compensate for a relatively meagre salary.

The cut belt found in the litter tray was the serial number expected from the stationary cupboard supply and was accompanied by a pair of rubber gloves. The gloves were still inside out from when they had been removed. DNA was extracted from the inside surfaces of them and proved to belong to Sheila Button. The outside surfaces had dark marks where they had gripped and pulled upon the belt, and analysis confirmed the substance. It could not, however, guarantee which particular belt had been seized.

The belt had a couple of whiskers off Sidney Button's beard but no fingerprints. There were also traces of latex from the gloves at both ends.

Confronted by such evidence, Sheila's solicitor advised her to plead guilty and cooperate with the police to get a shorter prison sentence. Accordingly, she was accompanied by him when she faced Webb and Newton in the interview room. After the recording equipment was switched on and the usual reminders about speaking under caution, Webb opened the interview:

"Tell me from the beginning about how this all happened, Mrs Button, please."

Sheila looked at her solicitor, who nodded. Then, she started to unravel the tale slowly at first before getting into her stride. It was almost as if she was repeating gossip about someone else:

"It all started with my Father-in-law Sidney. He was my boss at Button Manufacturing, and at first, I did not have much to do with him. Apart from ordering supplies and meeting reps, he never seemed to do much. Then Clive, his son and I got together. He had taken over from the old accountant that retired. He appeared to be happy in that was as far as he wanted to go in life, despite being more steady and better educated than his brother Gerry. So we got married, and I had ambitions for Clive to become the next Managing Director after his father. I intended to stay working for Button's until the first baby arrived, but that never happened.

It was evident that Gerry wasn't reliable, and he always seemed to me to be a bit of a playboy as I got to know him better. I don't think he was cut out for sales, but he wasn't interested in technical stuff like engineering either. At least my Clive made an effort to get a basic understanding of what happened on the factory floor. The daughter Gloria was OK, but I never had much contact with her other than handing out or collecting post. I could not see her as serious competition to lead the firm.

Anyway, as I said, it all started off with Sidney. He started to come and lean over me when I was at my desk, and I know he was trying to look down my blouse. It felt dirty and uncomfortable. He would brush past me without excuse, and I started to get frightened to take his tea into him after he patted my behind one day. I said 'No!' to him and fled. I tried to talk to Clive about it, but he just put me off: he said that his father was 'from another age' and 'that he didn't mean anything by it.' Clive's trouble is that he is afraid of confrontation and his Father. He has always been made to feel 'second best' against his older brother Gerry. I gather it was like that for Eric as well, being the younger brother of Sidney. Anyway, after that time he had patted my bottom, he stopped for a while. I mean, he was old enough to be my father, the dirty old pervert. Recently though, it all started up again, and he pushed himself against me as I left his office last Monday." Sheila paused for a sip of water.

"It must have been distressing, Sheila," said Ron encouraging her to go on. "What happened next?"

"Well, Gerry went to America to clinch an important deal. I don't know what went wrong, but Sidney called him into the office last Thursday and asked not to be disturbed. I was curious and listened from the corridor. Sidney was shouting at him, saying that he was lying and had let us all down. The last thing I heard was that he was threatening to sack him and told him to get out. I only just got back to my desk in time before I heard steps running down the stairs. I looked out of the kitchen window and saw Gerry roar away in that red car of his.

It struck me then that Eric and my Clive were the only ones in management that did any real work to keep that company going, and Eric had said he wouldn't fancy his brother's job. He prefers the technical side and apparently is very good at it. So I decided that I would have to take action myself: I waited until everybody was in their offices and went and got some gloves from the stationery cupboard. I put them on. Then I got a belt from the box and used my scissors to cut through it. It was harder than I thought, but I made it into one long strip eventually. Then I wiped the rubber marks off the scissors and put them back in the draw. I know that Sidney went downstairs for a while but heard him come back. I kept the gloves on and waited until Tim had gone into Clive's office. I know that they are usually in there for at least an hour when Tim goes in.

When I thought about what I had to do, I nearly backed out, but Sidney had made me so mad and disgusted that I went into his office without knocking. He was looking at the computer, and I stepped behind his chair without saying anything. I looped the belt around his neck, crossed it over and tugged hard with both hands. He tipped back in his chair a bit and was clawing at the belt, but he gave up quite quickly. When I was sure that he was dead, I left without looking back and closed the door. I went downstairs to Brunel's litter tray. I know that he never uses it – I think he must go outside somewhere. Anyway, I hid the belt and gloves under the litter. I didn't want to get caught with them on me, and the belt was a bit big to hide. I thought I could empty the whole tray into a paper sack on Tuesday night before leaving and put it into the dumpster. The binmen come every week on Wednesday morning before Tim arrives to unlock the place. I thought that nobody would look there, but you found it."

"Yes, we did, and you are the only person in the company that looks after Brunel", explained Webb. "The belt originated in the stationary cupboard because of its serial number, so it had to be someone who went in there. So what did you do after you had hidden the belt and gloves in the litter tray?"

"I tried to calm down and get my breath back before coming back upstairs. I waited nearly an hour, but nobody else went to visit Sidney, so I made his tea as usual and took it into his room. I didn't want to look at him, but I did. It made it easier to give a big scream and throw the mug of tea to the floor."

"Yes, I wondered how you had dropped it in fright without splashing your clothes," Webb interjected. "So what happened then?"

"Clive and Tim arrived first. Clive could see me in a state, so he held me tight for the first time in ages. He didn't know what I had been up to: it was just me. Tim went to look in the office and then came back to phone the police. By then, everyone else was crowding around. I think that you know the rest."

"Yes, it seems clear from there, thank you. This interview is being terminated at 3:14 pm on Tuesday 14th June 2016," announced DCI Webb.

After Sheila had been led away by a uniformed officer, Ron looked thoughtful and still sat in his interview seat. Eventually, he turned to Colin:

"Hearing her explain it all like that, it all sounded like one of those production lines for which they build the conveyor belts. There is a task that needs to be done in separate stages until the required product rolls off the end, in this case, the corpse of Sidney Button. Ordinary customers do not see the different processes, only the end result."

"That makes us Quality Control then, I guess," offered Colin.

Ron continued, ignoring the interjection. "You know, if Sheila had dumped the gloves in her wastepaper bin, we wouldn't have been able to connect them directly to the murder. Instead, she could have said that she had handled a belt to put into the post, and that was why her DNA was on them."

"Very true," reflected Colin. "Just as well, she confessed then," he added. "Careful, though."

"Why?"

"Solving a murder in less than a week. His Lordship is going to want that sort of productivity every time!" said Colin, joking.

"Many a true word said in jest!" retorted Ron grimly but smiled all the same.

Chapter 13

A few months after the Button murder, Colin Newton walked into his regular Ipswich gym and over to the treadmills. "Hello, this is a new one, isn't it?" he asked the trainer who was standing near it.

"Yes, all the gym group are getting upgrades and refurbishments. The old treadmills were not very reliable and broke down every few months. The plastic casings used to crack as well, but these look a lot sturdier. They were delivered from a local firm just up the road in Felixstowe." The cases of the new ones were made of aluminium, powder-coated in grey and looked very smart. Then Colin spotted a small badge, 'Button 3000 Treadmill, Felixstowe.' He smiled at the thought that the company had found something more popular to produce.

What had happened was that the apprentice Michael Dooley had gone to his regular gym, part of the same chain in Felixstowe. The staff had one of their treadmills on its side, looking underneath. "Burnt out!" said one of them in disgust.

"I bet we could build you a better one at where I work", ventured Michael Dooley.

"It can't be worse than this one. They take a fair hammering. They may be alright for light domestic use, but ours are going 12 hours a day sometimes," the manager said.

"If we built one, would you try it" Michael queried?

"Yes, it is a constant problem. I used to manage a branch of this company in Newcastle, and it was the same problem there."

The next day Michael sought out Tim and told him about the conversation. "Well, at least it's a type of conveyor belt, and we know how to build those. So tell you what, Michael, make a rough drawing, and we'll go and see Eric. You know we are desperate to come up with some more work."

The upshot was that with Eric's pooled brains and all the engineers' enthusiasm to save their jobs, a prototype was delivered to the gym in four weeks. The manager showed his boss, and they were satisfied that it was more rugged, quieter in operation and likely to be more reliable. A price was agreed to buy the machine and three more, which eventually led the chain to change over to the Button 3000 in all of their 78 gyms.

As Gerry had left Button Engineering to become an unsuccessful estate agent, Gloria handled the price and delivery negotiations with the gym chain from the marketing side of the company. She proved to be more hard-nosed in her role than her girlish good looks suggested, and soon the firm had better prospects. She also relished the challenge and certainly out-performed her brother, with no further thoughts of moving on.

In an unusual but popular move with the workers, Eric and Kathleen appointed Tim as the new CEO since Clive maintained that he did not want that responsibility and was of far more use as an accountant. He quietly put in divorce papers, sold his house and moved in with Tim. Despite their initial fears, they found that nobody cared who they fancied.

Kathleen has become an adventurous widow. She sold her home and the Bentley and bought a flat. She now enjoys cruises, driving and sending a succession of men wild. Gordon Barker was a bit too mouthy when sent to prison. As a result, he was beaten up and now feels that he is safer in solitary confinement. Sheila, facing a lengthy jail term, has settled into prison and wants to re-organise the library service, which she thinks is badly mismanaged.

About the author

Pete Jennings was born in Ipswich, Suffolk, in 1953. He has had careers as a telephone engineer, sales manager and recently retired as a registered social worker. He is also a registered psychotherapist and now lives on the Essex / Suffolk border. Some people are held up as shining examples to others, but Pete prefers to be an ominous warning.

Outside of his inner working life, Pete has sung with rock and folk bands, been a disco deejay and radio presenter, Anglo Saxon & Viking re-enactor, actor, folklorist, artist, ghost tour guide, storyteller & Pagan activist. He has had over twenty-five books published and regularly lectures in the UK and abroad.

He has a low boredom threshold, likes dogs, 70s prog rock, books, folk traditions, weird humour, real ale and wife Sue, but not necessarily in that order. One day he hopes to be recognised for his pioneering research on the Speed of Dark.

Pete regularly writes shorter magazine articles and reviews, especially for *Widowinde*, *Witchcraft & Wicca*, *Pagan Dawn* and *Pentacle*. He was also the editor of the *Gippeswic* magazine.

For the full expose of what he gets up to with incriminating photos see www.gippeswic.org

You can also follow Pete Jennings & *Ealdfaeder Anglo Saxons* on Facebook.

For appearances of Pete with his *Ealdfaeder Anglo Saxons* re-enactor friends, plus lots of information on Anglo Saxon topics, go to www.ealdfaeder.org

Other Books & eBooks by Pete Jennings

Pathworking (with Pete Sawyer) – Capall Bann (1993)
Northern Tradition Information Pack – Pagan Federation (1996)
Supernatural Ipswich – Gruff (1997)
Pagan Paths – Rider (2002)
The Northern Tradition – Capall Bann (2003)
Mysterious Ipswich – Gruff (2003)
Old Glory & the Cutty Wren – Gruff (2003)
Pagan Humour – Gruff (2005)
The Gothi & the Rune Stave – Gruff (2005)
Haunted Suffolk – Tempus (2006)
Tales & Tours – Gruff (2006)
Haunted Ipswich – Tempus/ History Press (2010)
Penda: Heathen King of Mercia and his Anglo-Saxon World. – Gruff (2013)
The Wild Hunt & its followers – Gruff (2013)
Blacksmith Gods, Myths, Magicians & Folklore – Moon Books- Pagan Portals (2014)
Heathen Information Pack (with others) – Pagan Federation (2014)
Confidently Confused – Gruff (2014)
Adventures in Ælphame – Gruff (2015)
Valkyries, selectors of heroes: their roles within Viking & Anglo-Saxon heathen beliefs. - Gruff (2016)
A Cacophony of Corvids: the mythology, facts, behaviour and folklore of ravens, crows, magpies and their relatives. - Gruff (2017)
Heathen Paths (2nd expanded & revised edition): Viking and Anglo-Saxon Pagan Beliefs – Gruff (2018)
The Bounds of Ælphame – Gruff (2019)
The Woodwose in Suffolk & beyond. – Gruff (2019)
Pathworking & Creative Visualisation – Gruff (2019)
Viking Warrior Cults – Gruff (2019)
When the sea turned to beer – Gruff (2020)
The Wyrd of Aelphame – Gruff (2020)
Dog Walk Detectives – Gruff (2021)
The Pagan Thinker – Gruff (2021)

Pete Jennings has also contributed to:
Modern Pagans: an investigation of contemporary Pagan practices. (Eds. V Vale & J. Sulak.) San Francisco, USA: RE/Search (2001)
The Museum of Witchcraft: A Magical History – (Ed. Kerriann Godwin) Boscastle: Occult Art Co. (2011)
Heathen Information Pack – UK: Pagan Federation (2014)
The Call of the God: an anthology exploring the divine masculine within modern Paganism (Ed. Frances Billinghurst) Australia: TDM (2015)
Pagan Planet: Being, Believing & Belonging in the 21st Century. Ed. Nimue Brown. UK: Moon Books (2016)

Recordings
Awake (with WYSIWYG) – Homebrew (1987)
Chocks Away (with WYSIWYG) Athos (1988)
No Kidding (with Pyramid of Goats) – Gruff (1990)
Spooky Suffolk (with Ed Nicholls) Gruff (2003)
Old Glory & the Cutty Wren CD – Gruff (2003)

Films that Pete has featured in
Suffolk Ghosts – Directed by Richard Felix. Past in Pictures, 2005
Wild Hunt – Directed by Will Wright. Film Tribe, 2006
In search of Beowulf with Michael Wood. BBC4, 2009
Born of Hope – Directed by Kate Maddison – Actors at Work 2009
The Last Journey – Directed by Carl Stickley, 2018

Find details of how to obtain these books and an up to date diary of lectures and appearances by Pete Jennings at www.gippeswic.org

All paperback books are available via my Veiled Market shop at
https://veiledmarket.com/product-category/books/?filter_vendor=87

Most books are also available in paperback and electronic digital versions via
www.amazon.co.uk/Pete-Jennings/e/B0034OPQP8